tuff ENOUGH

BLACKHAWK SECURITY BOOK 1

Happy Reading! ~Cole

SAMANTHA COLE

Suspenseful Seduction Publishing

Tuff Enough
Copyright ©2018 Samantha A. Cole
All Rights Reserved.
Suspenseful Seduction Publishing

Tuff Enough is a work of fiction. Names, characters, businesses, organizations, places, events, and incidents either are the product of the author's imagination or are used fictitiously. Any resemblance to actual persons, living or dead, events, or locales is entirely coincidental.

Editing by Eve Arroyo
Discreet cover by Samantha Cole
Sexy cover by Judi Perkins & Cover Me, Darlings

AI RESTRICTION: The author expressly prohibits any entity from using any part of this publication, including text and graphics, for purposes of training artificial intelligence (AI) technologies to generate text or graphics, including without limitation technologies that are capable of generating works in the same style or genre as this publication.
The author reserves all rights to license uses of this work for generative AI training and the development of machine learning language models.

No part of this book may be reproduced, scanned or distributed in any printed or electronic form without permission. Please do not participate in or encourage piracy of copyrighted materials in violation of the author's rights. Purchase only authorized editions.

AUTHOR'S NOTE

Any information regarding persons or places has been used with creative literary license so there may be discrepancies between fiction and reality. The missions and personal qualities of members of the military and law enforcement within have been created to enhance the story and, again, may be exaggerated and not coincide with reality.

The author has full respect for the members of the United States military and the varied members of law enforcement and thanks them for their continuing service to making this country as safe and free as possible.

CHAPTER ONE

Jason "Tuff" Tanner followed five operatives from Trident Security and his boss, Chase Dixon, as they descended the steps of the private jet to the tarmac of the small Albert Whitted Airport in St. Petersburg, Florida. They were returning from St. Lucia, where they'd been helping Ian Sawyer and another TS operative rescue their women and several others from a white-slavery syndicate. One of these days, Tuff would have to take a vacation down in the Caribbean. So far, the only times in his life he'd been to any of the islands had been work-related, so he'd never had a chance to do anything fun. Well, what other people would call fun. People who didn't get an adrenaline rush from their job or who weren't retired from any of the elite special-ops teams in the military like Tuff and the men he was currently with were. He'd done twelve years in the Army, with six of them in the 7th Special Forces Group, which was headquartered at Eglin Air Force Base in the Florida Panhandle. He lived for the missions that required him to use his training, instincts, prowess, and intelligence.

When they reached the parking lot, Tuff and Chase, the

owner of Blackhawk Security, said goodbye to Marco DeAngelis, Logan Reese, Kip Morrison, Jake Donovan, and Nick Sawyer, Ian's youngest brother. Tuff then turned to his boss. "Anything on the agenda tomorrow?"

Forty-two-year-old Chase Dixon was a retired Marine Raider. After leaving his military career behind, he started a private security company. Using his connections, experience, and business sense, he'd built Blackhawk into a thriving enterprise. His reputation was held in high regard throughout the United States and even beyond its borders. The good guys admired him, and the bad guys feared him.

Tuff had been working for Chase long enough to be no longer surprised when the man managed to come up with resources no one else seemed to be able to. Personnel, weapons, technology, transportation, etc.—whatever his associates and clients needed, Chase was able to provide. He'd made a fortune in government and private contracts and had dozens of operatives working for him, but there were still times the boss insisted on being on the front lines. Case in point, this last op. When he'd gotten the call for help from Ian, whom he considered a good friend, Chase had grabbed the first person he'd seen at the Blackhawk offices— Tuff, who'd been filling out a report on his latest case—and they'd hightailed it down to St. Lucia.

Now that the mission was over, the women were safe, a few perverted dirtbags were dead, and a chink in the sex-slave ring had been made. Unfortunately, there were more out there. But men like Tuff, Chase, the Sawyer brothers, and all their teammates would continue chipping away at organizations who preyed on the innocent until their dying day.

Chase ran a hand through his graying, short hair. "Nope. You've earned a few days off. You've been going nonstop for the past three months. Rest up. Find a soft, willing woman and have some wild, monkey sex. I don't want to see you at the office until next Monday's debriefing. Understood?"

"My momma didn't raise no fool. Monday it is. Thanks, Boss."

Without another word, Chase slapped Tuff on the shoulder and headed across the lot to his own vehicle. After tossing his duffel bag full of clothes, weapons, and gear into the narrow back seat of his F-150 pickup, Tuff climbed in behind the steering wheel. Starting it up, he cranked the AC up and lowered the windows to let out some of the stifling, hot air until it could be replaced. He wanted nothing more than to get home and into a refreshing shower before having a quick dinner and then sleeping for the next twenty-four hours.

Within twenty minutes, he'd navigated the last of the rush-hour traffic and pulled into his half of the driveway, next to a navy SUV, in front of the South Tampa duplex he lived in. Cutting off the engine, he climbed out of the truck and glanced around as he stretched out a few kinks that'd settled into his neck and back. It was a quiet neighborhood, just as he liked it. While he loved the excitement of his job, when he was home, he craved tranquility. A few kids lived on the cul-de-sac, but it was rare for them, or anyone else, to create a disturbance loud enough to bother him. Most kept their activities to their backyards, which reduced the chances of Tuff hearing them if he was trying to sleep during the day after an overnight or long mission.

He eyed the SUV. It belonged to his new next-door neighbor who'd moved in a few weeks ago. Due to his nonstop schedule over the past three months, Tuff had only met the woman a few times and mostly in passing. All he knew about the pretty thirty-something was her name was Concetta Suarez, but everyone called her "Chet," and she had curves that could knock a guy's eyes out of their sockets. She stood about five-foot-three, seven inches shorter than his height. Her Hispanic heritage shined through her beautiful caramel-toned skin, shiny black hair, and mink-colored eyes. She was a walking hard-on, coming and going, and if she hadn't lived right next door, Tuff definitely would have hit on her. But he knew better than to piss in his own sandbox.

Tuff wasn't a long-term relationship kind of guy. Even though he'd never lied about that to any woman he'd dated or even had a one-night-stand with, many of them had thought they could change him. When they couldn't, things usually hadn't ended well. If the sexy, little *bomboncita* next door turned out to be that type of woman, it would be hell living next to her if things went south. More than once, one of his ex-girlfriends or brief flings had shown up at his house, screaming like a banshee after he'd broken up with them. Twice, someone had needed to call the cops to restore quiet to the neighborhood. He could only imagine what would happen with a woman who lived in a home attached to his own. No thanks. He didn't want to have to give up the place he'd lived in for the past few years, nor did he want to get a restraining order against a neighbor. It was best to keep his hands to himself and his dick in his pants when it came to Chet.

After grabbing his duffel, Tuff climbed the few stairs to the shared front porch. As his gaze dropped to the keys in his hand, looking for the right one, the door to Chet's unit swung open. Without warning, a huge, muscular, tan pit bull lunged at Tuff, growling and barking. With quick reflexes honed over years of training and missions, Tuff dropped his duffel, vaulted over the banister, and landed on the balls of his feet in a flower bed, crushing several blooms.

"Meat! No! Stop! Easy, Meat!"

He was happy to see Chet had the beast on a leash but was worried she wouldn't be able to control "Meat" for long.

The dog's muscles strained as he tried to go after his quarry, and the woman holding him was clearly doing her best to prevent that from happening. Tuff readied himself to dive onto the hood of his truck. The last thing he wanted to do was draw the 9mm stuck in his back waistband and shoot the dog if it attacked, but he knew it might come down to that. Those snapping jaws could do irreparable damage to a person, even someone Tuff's size. It would destroy him if he had to put the dog down, though. He had a soft spot when it came to furry animals.

With the leather leash wrapped around her forearms, Chet lowered her voice to a soothing tone and maneuvered herself between the dog and his target. "Easy, boy. It's okay. He's not going to hurt you. Easy."

Tuff prayed the woman knew what she was doing as the dog kept trying to see around her to the man he wanted to rip apart. Meat's massive chest heaved as he panted and growled while drool rolled down his jowls.

"Eh!" The sharp sound of Chet's voice grabbed the dog's attention, and when he looked up at her, she continued in her calming voice, "Good boy. That's a good boy."

She waved her hand in front of the canine's nose. It took a moment, but the scent of whatever she was holding seemed to register and catch his interest.

"Meat, sit." She tugged on the leash once while making some sort of hand signal, and, thank God, the damn thing finally obeyed, sitting on its haunches, no longer interested in tearing into Tuff's hide—at least for the moment. After the silence remained for a count of three, she rewarded the dog with the food in her hand. Slobbering all over the porch, the dog barely chewed before swallowing.

Petting the pit's massive head, Chet murmured a few times before turning to look at Tuff apologetically. "I'm so sorry about that. I didn't know you were out here. Meat's had a tough life so far, and he's very wary of men."

Tuff relaxed a little and snorted. "If that's wary, I'd hate to see when he gets hostile."

Still stroking the dog, Chet frowned. "That's what happens to pit bulls when they're raised from puppies to be fight dogs."

"Fight dog? Is he from the raid I heard about last week?" He remembered her telling him she was an animal control officer for Hillsborough County, which included the city of Tampa, and volunteered with rescue groups.

"Yeah. He and fourteen others. They were found caged in a warehouse in deplorable conditions. Two had been so badly injured they had to be euthanized." She clearly wasn't happy about that, and Tuff didn't blame her.

Studying the dog, now that Meat wasn't trying to kill him, Tuff could see the multiple scars that covered his face and body. His velvet-covered ears had been cropped, and there was a cleft on the side of his upper lip from a tear that'd healed without stitches. Despite the damage, he was a beautiful dog, and Tuff wished he could spend five minutes alone with the bastards who'd used Meat and the other dogs for sport. No animal should be abused in any way, shape, or form.

"Sorry to hear that. So, he's staying with you?" Renters were allowed pets as long as there weren't any complaints from the neighbors about them.

"I'm fostering him for now. We bonded at the shelter. Once he was out of quarantine, I brought him home to show him what it was like to be pampered. He'd never seen the inside of a house or had a soft bed before. I'm hoping to retrain him so he can find a forever home."

Tuff's gaze dropped to Meat, who'd finally laid down on

the concrete, still panting, then returned to Chet's face. "That'll probably take a while."

Her chin lifted. "I think he's worth it."

"I didn't think he wasn't." He scratched his temple. Tuff loved all animals, but dogs especially. He'd had a few while growing up, and there'd been some in his Army unit. When they weren't working, he and his buddies had enjoyed playing fetch with the MWDs, or just sitting there, petting them. "Can I help?"

Chet's head tilted to the side. "How?"

"You can use me to get him to understand not all men want to harm him. Think if I lay down on the grass, you can let him sniff me? I'll stay perfectly still. Then you can reward him when he doesn't sink his teeth into me."

"Um . . . yeah, if you don't mind. I'll walk him around you, but not too close."

"Great." Tuff headed for the middle of the lawn in front of Chet's side of the house, wondering if he'd just signed himself up to be the dog's next meal.

CHAPTER TWO

Chet watched as her tattooed neighbor lay on the grass beside the driveway. When she'd met Jason Tanner a few weeks ago, she'd immediately had some stereotypical wariness about the man. His thick muscles were the first thing she'd noticed about him, followed by the colorful tattoos that covered his arms and peeked out from the V-necked shirt he'd been wearing at the time. She'd been worried she'd moved in next door to some biker dude with a rap sheet as long as her arm. His friendly smile and twinkling blue eyes, which were currently covered by his sunglasses, had helped her relax a little as he politely introduced himself and welcomed her to the neighborhood. After a few minutes of back-and-forth, new-acquaintance conversation between them, she'd felt more of her concern ebb.

He'd mentioned he'd been in the military and now worked as a bodyguard and private investigator. When she'd stated she was an animal control officer with the county, he'd asked if she knew Kat Michaelson, which she did. Kat was a local K9 trainer for the state police and Tampa P.D. She also trained dogs for private security. Apparently, Jason's employer was one of those companies who'd contracted Kat and her growing staff.

That first day had been the only time Chet had engaged in a conversation with Jason that'd lasted more than a minute since usually one of them was coming home as the other was leaving when they ran into each other. From what she'd learned from her other neighbors, Jason was well-liked, didn't cause any problems on the street, and occasionally played basketball with the kids on the block. He was also quick to offer his help to anyone who needed it when he was home. His job took him out of town a lot. One of the men on the block was a St. Petersburg police officer, and another was a Tampa fireman. They kept an eye on Jason's house for him whenever he was away on an assignment for a few days. Chet liked how her new neighbors looked out for each other. It made her feel better about her hasty decision to rent her half of the duplex.

Pushing the thoughts of why she'd needed to find a new place to live from her mind, she gave Meat's leash a firm tug. "*Stehen.*" The German command for stand was pronounced *sch-stay-en*. Since the bastards involved in the fight club had used English and some Spanish commands, she wanted to break Meat's habit of responding to them. Earlier, she'd been so startled when she'd opened her door to see Jason and the pittie had lunged for him that she'd spoken English to the dog. But now that she was in training mode, Chet switched back to German, which was often used for training protection canines. It wasn't a common language in the US, so it was less likely a criminal or anyone else would know the proper commands to get a dog to do what they wanted.

The big meatball looked up at her, his tongue lolling from the side of his mouth. His name definitely fit him. She waited a moment, then repeated her command. "Meat, stehen."

This time he pushed himself up and stood next to her leg.

He was a work-in-progress and would be for a while, but he was slowly learning that he was rewarded when he obeyed her. Chet patted his ribs. *"Braver Hund."* Good dog.

Making sure she had a firm grip on the leash, she ordered Meat to heel and walk beside her as she gave the leash another tug. *"Fuss."*

They descended the stairs, and Chet stopped a few feet onto the grass and ordered the dog to sit. Again, when Meat hesitated, she waited a moment, then used one of his treats to entice him into obeying.

There were about seven feet between them and Jason, who was lying face down, his hands under his chin. His T-shirt and cargo pants hugged his torso and ass, making her mouth water. He was a fine-looking specimen of the male gender. While he looked very relaxed, she didn't doubt he could move quickly if needed to avoid getting bit—not that Chet would let Meat get that close to him. At least, not today.

Keeping a safe distance, she slowly walked Meat around the prone man, who stayed perfectly still. The canine's nose was sniffing a mile a minute. Each time, after they'd circled around to Jason's feet, Chet had Meat sit, then praised him and gave him a small piece of the beef jerky he loved. She then moved a little closer to Jason and repeated the process. After giving Meat his reward following the third rotation, Chet had him heel then follow to her car. "You can get up now, but not too quickly."

Slowly, Jason got to his feet. "That went well."

"It did. Thank you so much, but it'll take a lot more time before he doesn't feel threatened by you." It also didn't mean Meat would be relaxed around any man other than Jason, but maybe in time, the dog would be okay with having a male in his forever home.

"That's okay. I'm off work until Monday, and I'll just be catching up on a few things around the house, so if you want to do that a couple of times a day, just knock. Hopefully, he'll start feeling comfortable around me and won't feel the need to try to take a chunk out of my ass every time he sees me."

Chet chuckled. It would be a major loss to all women if Jason Tanner had a chunk missing from that fine ass. "Thanks."

"You're welcome." He gestured toward the house. "Let me hit the shower and grab something to eat. It's been a long day."

"Sure. Thanks again."

He nodded, then keeping a good distance between himself and Meat, he ambled toward the stairs. Chet's gaze was pinned on him from his waist down. When he reached the porch, he snatched his duffel bag from where he'd dropped it earlier, then turned around and waved at her. His amused grin told her he'd caught her staring at his ass. Heat bloomed across her cheeks as she yanked on the driver's door handle to find she hadn't unlocked it yet. By the time she pulled the keys out from the pocket of her jeans, then unlocked and opened the door, Jason had disappeared into his half of the duplex.

Chet sighed as she eyed the dog at her feet. "I've sworn off males of the human species, Meat. And even if I hadn't, getting involved with a guy I live next door to is never a good idea, so it's just you and me. Okay?"

As if he'd understood her every word, the canine let loose a hearty "woof."

CHAPTER THREE

For the third time that week, Tuff awoke to an erotic dream featuring his next-door neighbor, his hand around his aching cock, and her name on his lips. Damn, she was making it hard to keep things platonic between them. Not that she'd indicated she was interested in him. Nope, she'd kept things friendly. And she'd kept her distance. Well, that probably had to do with Meat. Twice a day, Tuff had met the canine and handler in the backyard—Chet hadn't wanted any distractions like one of the neighborhood kids riding by on a bike or a delivery truck pulling in.

Meat had relaxed enough over the past six days to sniff Tuff up close and personal. Chet had set little treats along his shoulders, back, and legs. At first, the dog was hesitant, but Tuff stayed perfectly still as each little morsel was eaten. Slowly, he was earning the dog's trust.

Since Tuff had to report back to work today, they wouldn't have a chance to do the routine until later in the day. While he loved his downtime, six days were too long for him not to be doing anything exciting. But it had given him plenty of time to get stuff done around the house. Even though he rented—his cousin owned the duplex—Tuff did much of the maintenance and upkeep for both units. He'd told his cousin he'd only move in if his rent covered half the mortgage, taxes, and all the utilities for his side. Money was tight for Taylor and his family right now, and if the two rentals didn't at least break even, he'd have to sell the property he'd inherited from his maternal grandmother. That was why Tuff fixed whatever he could around the place.

Flinging the sheets off his nude body, Tuff stood and strode to the bathroom. He was due at the Blackhawk offices at 8:00 a.m., which gave him an hour to shower, stop for coffee and an egg-white sandwich, and get to the building that housed the security business in St. Petersburg. After talking to one of his teammates last night, he didn't expect anything big to be on the agenda this week. But that was always subject to change in the blink of an eye.

Like Trident Security, Blackhawk had several government contracts, and the operatives never knew when they'd get a call to go wheels up to another part of the world, usually with less than an hour's notice. Especially since they contracted out to other companies like Trident. Tuff liked working with those guys. They were a fun bunch, even though the original six had all been Navy SEALs. While their new Omega team was an eclectic mix of people coming from different military branches or law enforcement, the Alpha team still liked to sling shit about SEALs being the best of the best. Three-on-three basketball games at their compound tended to result in plenty of bruises and a few drops of blood being spilled, but it was all in the name of a healthy, friendly rivalry. The operatives of Trident knew those from Blackhawk had their backs when shit got real and vice versa. Tuff trusted the Sawyers and their teams as much as he trusted his own teammates and boss.

Fifty minutes later, a little bummed he hadn't seen Chet

when he'd left the house, Tuff entered the five-story building that housed the headquarters for BHS. While the "h" was lowercase and in the middle of the word Blackhawk, having BS for the company's initials wouldn't exactly instill confidence in new clients, so the uppercase "H" had been added to the logo.

After passing through security, while bypassing the metal detectors for those who weren't authorized to carry, Tuff headed to the elevators and rode one to the fourth floor with several other operatives, all going to the same morning briefing. He followed the small crowd into a huge room that looked like a movie theater. The sloped floor and rows of comfortable, plush seats accommodated up to fifty operatives and allowed a good view of the front of the room. Each seat had a folding tabletop tucked under an armrest, like airline trays, that could be pulled out and used to lean on while taking notes. Taking a seat in the middle, Tuff set his coffee in a cup holder attached to the end of the armrest.

At the front of the room was a 120-foot screen separated into sections to accommodate twenty different video feeds. At the moment, only six of them were showing images from current ops in progress. Directly under the screen was a computer setup worthy of NASA—and that wasn't even the main system. *That* monstrosity was located on the third floor.

Sitting in front of the computer was a blonde-haired woman named Bianca Gordon—hacker extraordinaire. Nicknamed Gordo, she gave Brody "Egghead" Evans over at Trident a run for his money sometimes. It wasn't unheard of for the two geeks to challenge each other in hacking competitions. Tuff wasn't sure what they hacked into and had no desire to know. Plausible deniability was always a good thing to have in some situations, and that was one of them.

Blane "Boots" Nelson plopped down in the seat next to

Tuff, yawning as he did so. Tuff glanced at the other operative he'd been partnered with numerous times. His eyes were red, and it was obvious he was having a hard time keeping them open.

Tuff let out a snort. "Jesus, dude, you look like crap. When was the last time you slept?"

Checking his military-style wristwatch, Blane responded, "Six weeks, five days, and fourteen hours ago—give or take an hour."

Tuff laughed. Almost seven weeks ago, his buddy's wife had given birth to their second child, Jonah—otherwise known as Satan's spawn because the kid was colicky and still wasn't sleeping during the night.

Before either could say anything more, a loud rapping of knuckles against wood came from the front of the room. Chase was standing behind the room's podium. "All right. Let's get to work. Jester, where are you and Minx on the Piedmont case?"

"Up a fucking creek without a paddle." Jerry "Jester" Beekman was sitting four rows ahead of Tuff, yet the man's booming voice easily carried to those behind him. His partner, Lucy "Minx" Ward, sat next to him.

"That's not what I want to hear."

"That's not what I want to report, either, but there it is." A few chuckles filled the room at the sarcasm in his voice. The bear of a man rattled off all the things that had gone wrong so far on the case they'd been assigned. Two months ago, a local businessman had been shot and killed, and after the police had failed to come up with any leads, the man's brother had hired Blackhawk to investigate the homicide.

"So we suspect the killer has ties to Tampa P.D.?" Chase asked while frowning. The man hated when the supposed good guys turned out to be the bad guys.

"Starting to look that way—just not sure to what extent—

could be a friend or relative of an OTJ . . ." That was law-enforcement speak for someone on-the-job. ". . . but whoever it is covered their tracks. We have a lead that came in late last night that we'll follow up on, but if it doesn't pan out, I'm not sure where the hell to go from here." He glanced at his partner for confirmation, and she nodded.

"All right. Keep me posted. If you hit another brick wall, come back here, and Irv and I will do a debrief with both of you. Maybe something will pop up that was overlooked."

Lance Irving had been Chase's righthand man for several years now and often took part in the bull sessions that were needed for the more difficult or intricate cases. Some people might be insulted if their boss indicated they might've missed something, but unless it was stupidly obvious, Chase never called his operatives out on it. He always said that sometimes it just took a fresh set of eyes to look things over. No one was perfect—even him. That attitude had earned him the respect of every person who'd ever worked for him.

As the meeting dragged on, one by one, the individual operatives or teams gave updates on their current cases, if they were on one, and then Chase began to dole out new assignments. Tuff straightened in his seat when he heard his name called. "Tuff, Boots, Corndog, and Sherlock, the Dali Museum has a loaned exhibit flying in. We'll provide extra security during the transport from the airport to the museum tonight. Sherlock, you've got the lead on that. I requested the same museum personnel as last time to be involved since everything went like clockwork. The curator, Sherrie Kirk, is your contact again."

Tuff's phone vibrated with an incoming text. He didn't bother to look at it since he knew Gordo had just sent him and the three others all the details about the assignment. After the briefing ended, the foursome would meet to review everything together. It was an easy gig, one they'd done numerous times for local museums or businesses, but that didn't mean they could be lax about it. The one time that happened was the one time everything would go FUBAR. While art heists weren't very common in the Tampa/St. Petersburg area, they could be lucrative for thieves. In some circles, works by Salvador Dali were the holy grail. A heist would have to involve a lot of planning, so the security team needed to be able to thwart those plans with some of their own.

Ten minutes later, the briefing ended, and everyone filed out of the room, ready to work on their assignments. Tuff and his teammates spent the next hour and a half in one of the conference rooms, plotting the route they'd take from the airport to the museum, among other details. They never took the same route twice, and each one was subject to change at the drop of a hat if something didn't feel right. Once they'd nailed down each component of the assignment, Tuff headed to the second floor and zig-zagged through the maze of cubicles belonging to Blackhawk's operatives before arriving at his own and taking a seat. While his computer booted up, he sifted through the stack of mail that'd been left on his desk, tossing out anything that was junk. Next, he tackled his email, filtering out what he needed and deleting the rest. Finally, he got down to the reports he had to finish writing and a few things he wanted to research online.

Arching his back to loosen the kinks that appeared more often as of late, he was surprised to see it was just past 1:00 p.m. No wonder his stomach was growling. Standing, he pushed the chair under the desk and grabbed his keys and phone. On his way out to find some lunch, a thought occurred to him. Maybe he'd stop in the butcher shop next to the pizzeria across the street and pick up a few bones for Meat. They say the way to a man's heart is through his stomach—maybe it was true for male canines too.

CHAPTER FOUR

Just after 1:00 a.m., Tuff turned into his cul-de-sac, looking forward to climbing into bed. The transport gig had taken longer than usual because the plane had been late. A strong storm system over LaGuardia airport in New York had resulted in numerous flights being delayed. Tuff doubted anybody on the commercial flight had known that millions of dollars in art had been safely stowed in the cargo hold of their 757.

Curator Sherrie Kirk and her assistant had overseen the crates being transferred from the plane to a large truck by vetted employees of the airport and a moving company the museum had on contract. When the caravan arrived at its destination, museum employees were waiting to help unload and catalog each crate. All this had been done under the watchful eyes of the heavily-armed Blackhawk team and museum security guards. The route from the airport to the museum had been one of three that'd been planned out and selected at random moments before they left the tarmac. After everything had been locked in the museum's huge walk-in vault and the building's alarm system had been reset, Tuff and the rest of the team had been able to head home.

As he pulled into his shared driveway next to Chet's vehicle, the headlights on his truck illuminated her side of the duplex. Tuff immediately went into combat mode when he saw a dark figure dart around the corner of the house. Throwing his truck into park, he opened the driver's door and leaped out, taking off after the unidentified person. The chain-link fence around the side of the house rattled as if someone had swung open the gate or vaulted over it. Tuff didn't remember pulling his weapon from its holster at his hip, but muscle memory could do that. All he knew was the gun was in his hand, locked and loaded, safety off, and the heavy weight reassuring.

After checking and ensuring he wasn't running into an ambush, Tuff rounded the corner and pushed open the metal gate. From inside Chet's unit, Meat was going ballistic, barking his head off. Hopefully, the dog wouldn't crash through a window to go after whoever Tuff was chasing—or even Tuff, for that matter. When he reached the backyard, Tuff saw the suspect jump over the rear fence onto the property of the people who lived one street over and keep going.

The trained operative quickly closed the distance between himself and the fence and vaulted over it. The roar of an engine and screeching tires reached his ears as he took off at a sprint again. When he ran out into the street, all he saw were the taillights of a dark-colored SUV, possibly a Cadillac Escalade, as it made a left turn onto the main street. There was far too little moonlight or streetlight and the distance too great for Tuff to see the license plate.

"Shit!" His nostrils flared, and his heart raced as he stared at the entrance to the cul-de-sac. A few moments passed before he turned and headed back to the duplex the same way he'd come, through the neighbor's yard and over the fence, holstering his weapon once again.

At some point, the lights had been turned on outside Chet's back and front doors, so Tuff knew she was awake, which was expected after the racket Meat had made. Now, though, the dog was silent.

After striding around from the back of the house to the front, Tuff stopped short when he saw the driver's side of Chet's car. The word "bitch" had been spray painted in huge letters across both the front and rear doors, and he wondered who the hell she'd pissed off. An ex-boyfriend or her ex-husband, perhaps? He'd learned she was divorced during one of their conversations while working on getting Meat comfortable around him. While she hadn't elaborated, Tuff had gotten the impression her marriage hadn't ended well.

Needing to know she was safe, Tuff climbed the stairs and knocked on Chet's door.

"Who is it?" Her response was immediate as Meat started up again. "*Ruhig*, Meat."

"It's Tuff," he told her, loud enough for her to hear over the barking. "Open the door, Chet."

It took a few moments and a repeated command before the dog quieted again. "Hang on."

A thump, like something heavy hitting wood just inside the door, was followed by the lock being flipped. The door swung open. Chet stood before him with a leash in her hand attached to Meat's collar. She held it close to the side of the dog's neck, preventing any attempts at lunging forward. Beside her in the foyer was an entry table with a Ruger 9mm, compact enough to fit easily in the woman's smaller hands sitting on it. He was happy to see she had a way to protect herself, although he doubted Meat would let any harm come to his mistress.

Surprisingly, the big dog's tail thumped against the tiled floor when he spotted Tuff, which reminded the man he had some beef bones in his refrigerator for the animal. But they'd have to wait. His eyes roamed over Chet's body, and it didn't take a genius to figure out she wasn't wearing a bra under the thin nightshirt, which stopped right above her knees. Below that, her legs and feet were bare. It was difficult to do, but Tuff forced his gaze to her face. "Are you okay, Chet?"

"Yeah, I'm fine. But what the hell is going on?"

"You tell me. I pulled up to see someone dressed in black running from your car. I chased after him or her, but they got away. I get back here and see your car's been spray painted." When her eyes grew wide in disbelief, he cocked his head toward the stairs. "Come take a look."

"Someone spray-painted my car?" Without putting anything on her feet, she stepped toward him, and Tuff moved aside to let her and Meat exit the house. She kept the big dog on the opposite side of her, away from Tuff, and then hurried down the stairs.

When she caught sight of the damage, she cried out in dismay. "My car! Who—who the hell . . . why would someone do this?" Her gaze flitted to Tuff, who stood nearby with his arms crossed. "You didn't get a good look at them?"

"Nope. Black hoodie, black pants, black sneakers, about five feet ten, a hundred-and-sixty pounds. I'll check the security camera aimed at my door and the backyard—" He'd also add a few more cameras aimed at her door, windows, and the entire driveway by tomorrow evening. "—but I'm not optimistic about getting a better description than that. Any idea who you pissed off? An ex?"

She stiffened for a moment, then shook her head. "No. There haven't been any boyfriends for a while, and it's not my ex-husband."

"You're sure?"

"Unless you got the description wrong, he's six-three and over two hundred pounds, so, yeah, I'm sure."

Tuff wasn't convinced. "He could've hired someone to do this."

"Either way, it would violate the order of protection—he has to stay away from me, and so far, he has."

His eyes narrowed. "Why do you have an OP against him?"

Chet took a deep breath and looked down at the dog sitting next to her. "It's not important because it wasn't him. Let me call the police. *Fuss*, Meat." This time the canine didn't hesitate to follow the command to heel.

Tuff ground his molars together but didn't push Chet for more information than she was willing to give right now. Although they seemed to be getting along this past week, there was still a lot they didn't know about each other. He didn't want her to think he was being nosy. Besides, there were other ways he could find out about her ex-husband.

For now, he'd wait for the police with her, so he could give his statement. Then, tomorrow, he'd start on a list of things he needed to do to ensure Chet's safety. He'd be damned if anything happened to her on his watch.

CHAPTER FIVE

"Thank you for coming, officers," Chet said as she escorted the two uniformed men to her front door. "I appreciate it."

"No worries, ma'am," the taller one responded. "We'll take a few photos of your car before we leave. You can call your insurance company in the morning and give them the report number I gave you." He'd given her his department business card with the information on it.

"Thank you, I will. Have a good night." She closed the door behind them, then walked back into her kitchen, where Tuff was still drinking a cup of decaf coffee she'd made while waiting for the police. He was doing something on his laptop, which he'd brought over from his place to show the officers the video from his security system. While he'd been grabbing that, Chet had taken a few moments to run into her bedroom and change out of her thin nightshirt, replacing it with a sports bra, a T-shirt, and sweatpants.

With the police gone, Chet was torn between wanting Tuff to leave or stay. For now, she went with the latter, especially since he'd done something really sweet. Meat was currently lying down just over the dining room threshold, gnawing on a huge bone Tuff had brought him before the police had arrived. Tuff had sat quietly on the kitchen floor, crossed his ankles, and held the tasty treat out to the dog. At first, Meat had hesitated, but it wasn't long before the temptation had drawn him closer. Tuff's gaze had been focused on his lap, so he didn't appear to be challenging the canine. After a few moments of soft whining and dancing from side to side, Meat had stretched his neck out and gently taken the proffered bone. Then, surprising both humans, the dog had plopped down about a foot away from Tuff and enjoyed his treat. That was until the doorbell sounded.

Once Chet had the barking Meat under control again, Tuff had gotten to his feet and let the cops in. The dog then retreated under the dining room table, where Chet had followed and given him the bone once more. After realizing the uniformed men were remaining in the kitchen, Meat finally relaxed and even moved out from under the table.

Picking up her empty cup, Chet stepped over to the coffeepot and refilled it. Leaning against the counter and sipping the dark brew, she studied her neighbor. Why did the man have to be so damn sexy? She would've settled for him just being a nice guy, but add in his muscular physique, gorgeous ink, and handsome face, and Chet knew she was in trouble. She'd been having erotic dreams about him all week. Of course, it didn't help that it'd been over a year since she'd had sex. Billy-Bob, her vibrator, just wasn't satisfying her enough lately. Maybe that was why she got all tingly whenever Tuff was around. Aside from some teasing and mild flirting, though, he hadn't given her any indication he was interested in her other than as a friend and neighbor, and she wasn't sure she wanted him to.

"Are you okay?"

His words penetrated Chet's brain, and she realized she

was staring at him. Pushing off the counter, she sat across the table from him. "I'm mad, nervous, and bewildered, all wrapped up in one tired package, but yeah, I'll be okay. I just can't figure out why I was targeted."

Tuff shrugged those sculpted shoulders of his—the black T-shirt he wore did nothing to hide their contours. "Could be something as obscure as you cut someone off while driving or some guy with a secret crush who you inadvertently snubbed. Or . . . it could be someone you know all too well." He crossed his arms on the table and leaned forward. His tone was gentle when he said, "Tell me about your ex-husband, Chet. Why do you have an OP against him? And don't tell me it doesn't matter because you don't think it's him. Security and protection are what I do, and I can't help you if I don't know everything."

When they'd arrived, the police officers had already known about the order of protection. Apparently, it popped up on their car computer because it was associated with her address. She hadn't needed to go into detail about it, but she'd told them she didn't think Roland would do something so petty. He preferred to use his fist, a fact she'd found out only two months after their wedding, following a six-month courtship. Chet had always said she would never be one of those women who'd stick around after a man had hit them, but she'd fallen into the trap she now knew all about. The one where he would apologize and treat her like gold for a while until the next time he flew off the handle.

While many women never managed to escape the cycle, Chet had decided after the third time Roland had hit her that there wouldn't be a fourth. Thankfully, she had some friends who'd helped her move out one day while he'd been at work. The very next day, her husband had been served with divorce papers and the order of protection her lawyer had requested on her behalf. There'd been several times Roland had called her since then, despite the OP, trying to convince her to come back to him, but she'd refused to answer his calls, sending them straight to voicemail. The only time he'd come knocking, after finding out where she'd been living with a friend a few months ago, she'd met him at the door with one of her rescued pit bulls and her gun. When she didn't back down, he finally realized she was serious, and there was no way in hell she'd forgive and forget. He hadn't contacted her since.

Biting her upper lip, Chet hesitated. She was ashamed she'd stayed with her ex after the first time he'd hit her, but something about Tuff had her opening her mouth and spilling her guts. "I was married to Roland Stratford."

His eyes narrowed. "As in the mayor of St. Petersburg's brother?"

"Yup, that would be him." She let out a heavy sigh. "Looking back, I knew we were rushing into things. I'm embarrassed to admit I got swept up in the wining and dining and the fancy parties. We'd only been dating a few months when he proposed, and like a fool, I said yes."

Reaching across the table, Tuff laid his hand over hers. "The last thing I'd call you is a fool, Chet. People make mistakes all the time, it's a part of life. We learn from them and move on. Did you love him?"

She shrugged as her cheeks heated in shame. Why she was telling him all this, she didn't know, but he really was easy to talk to. "I thought I did, but now I know I really didn't. I had second thoughts that whole week leading up to the wedding, but I just thought all women have the jitters right before they get married. I've heard my friends and family say they'd had them, and their marriages all turned out well for the most part, so I just brushed it off and said, 'I do.'"

"What happened after that?"

Her gaze was pinned on the table in front of her. She couldn't say the words.

"Did he hit you, Chet?"

Tears rolled down her cheeks, and she nodded.

Tuff let out a muttered curse. Without letting go of her hand, he stood and circled around to her side of the table. Once he was there, he put one arm behind her back, and the other under her knees, then lifted. Startled, she squeaked and grabbed onto his broad shoulders, but all he did was take her seat and set her down on his lap. He wrapped his arms around her and snuggled her against his hard chest. As if sensing Chet needed him too, Meat padded into the kitchen and stopped about a foot in front of her and Tuff. He bowed his basketball-sized head and whined, clearly unsure about approaching them further. Instead of using the "come" command, Chet put her hand palm up and gestured with her fingers for him to come closer. After a few hesitant steps, he moved to her side, in front of Tuff's knees, and settled his big head on her thigh. She ran her hand down his neck and back, reassuring him as much as he was comforting her. A few moments later, Tuff slowly raised his hand and scratched the dog's ears. It was a small miracle that Meat allowed it, but Chet was too busy crying to celebrate.

There she sat, in Tuff's lap, with Meat's head in her own, letting them soothe her. She'd shed many tears the three times Roland had hit her, but since then, she'd tried to tell everyone and herself she wouldn't cry over him anymore. Even now, it wasn't about him. These tears were for her naivety back then—before and after the wedding. She should've turned him down when he'd proposed. She should've listened to her gut when it'd screamed at her to run the night before the wedding. She should've taken a baseball bat to his hands the first time he'd hit her and never given him the opportunity to do it again.

CHAPTER SIX

As he held Chet in his arms, Tuff mentally field-stripped every weapon he'd ever fired, either in target practice or during a live mission, to keep from growing hard against her hip. His heart and mind had wanted to comfort her when he'd set her on his lap, but his damn dick had other fucking plans. Thank God she'd changed into a T-shirt and sweats before the cops had arrived. Not only would Tuff have been jealous as fuck that any other man was seeing her dressed in her nightshirt sans bra, but if she still had it on now, he would've been so tempted to dip his hand under the hem of it. While she'd stopped crying and was currently resting her head on his shoulder, now was definitely not the time to let her know he was interested in getting to know her much, much better.

His thoughts flitted to her ex-husband. While he didn't know the businessman personally, Tuff knew who he was. Roland Stratford had stood by his brother's side, supporting him through two successful campaigns for the mayor's office. Roland would be very lucky if he never ran into Tuff because, right now, he wanted to hunt the bastard down and beat the ever-living shit out of him. It killed Tuff, knowing any man had laid an unkind hand on Chet. No woman deserved that, especially not one he was starting to have feelings for—feelings that went beyond wanting her in his bed.

A loud groan came from Meat as Tuff scratched his ears, and the man chuckled softly. He was still shocked the dog was letting him touch him—the friendship bone must've made an impression on the big lug. While Tuff knew he still had to move slowly when the dog was near, this was a step in the right direction.

Chet stirred, and when she tried to stand, Tuff let her as Meat meandered over to his water bowl for a drink. His mistress wiped away the remnants of her tears and looked at Tuff. "I'm sorry about that. I'm not usually a crier."

Reaching out, he took her hand and squeezed it. "No need to apologize. Anytime you need a shoulder, feel free to borrow mine."

The corners of her mouth ticked upward. "Thanks." She glanced at something behind him, and her eyes went wide. "Oh, my God. It's three o'clock. You have to be exhausted. I should let you go get some sleep."

He wanted to tell her that no matter how tired he was, he wasn't ready to leave yet but knew it was in her best interest to step back and give her a little space. Tuff got to his feet. "You should go to bed too." Picking up his laptop, he headed for the front door with her and Meat trailing in his wake. "Lock up behind me and keep your gun close." Thankfully, because of her job, she had a conceal-carry license for the weapon and knew how to use it. "I'll take another walk around the property, then tomorrow I'll get a few more cameras set up." She'd argued with him about that earlier, but he'd been firm. It wouldn't be too difficult to add to the system he already had set up.

"Please let me know what it will cost, and I'll pay for them."

He came up short and frowned at her. "Did you forget what I do for a living? We have hundreds of these cameras. I get them for free, so there's no charge." Actually, that was a small lie—he got them for cost—but he didn't want her worrying about that. "Besides, if there were, I'd just take it off next month's rent." Another small lie. "My cousin is good about stuff like that. Now, lock up behind me."

Before he could turn toward the door, Chet stopped him with a hand on his bicep. "Tuff?"

He raised his brow at her.

"Thank you. For . . . everything."

The warmth, gratitude, and something he couldn't name that he saw in her eyes melted his resolve. He cupped her cheek, and when that warmth flared to molten lava, he leaned down and brushed his lips against hers. She tasted like coffee and pure sin, and it took everything inside him not to deepen the kiss. Straightening again, he stared at her startled but heated expression. His voice was a raspy whisper when he said, "You're welcome."

"Yoo-hoo! Chet! Anybody home?"

Chet shook her head, trying to clear it. Her mind had gone to the same place it'd been wandering to all day—to that moment when she realized Tuff was going to kiss her, and then he did. But before she could get over her shock and respond, he'd walked out the door. Now, she couldn't forget how his lips had felt against hers, nor that she wanted him to kiss her again. But was she reading too much into the moment? Maybe he'd just meant it as a kiss between friends. But she could swear she'd seen desire in his eyes as he pulled away from her, and friends usually didn't kiss each other on the lips.

"Hey, Chet, are you okay?"

Dragging herself back to the present, she looked at Tori Freyja, the head trainer and founder of Healing Heroes, a local charity that rescued dogs and trained them to be service/assistant companions for veterans with PTSD. Quite a few of the dogs Chet had rescued from poor environments over the last few years had graduated from Tori's program and were now in forever homes with veterans. Chet had driven to the small ranch Tori owned, just north of Tampa, with two dogs she'd pulled from the shelter to see if they had the right temperament and instincts to go through the program. Meat had also made the trip but was currently in the office with Tori's assistant, relaxing in the air conditioning.

Once more, Chet shook the cobwebs from her mind. "Huh?"

Tori laughed at her as she stood in the middle of the fenced-in training field. "Where'd you go? I called your name four times."

"Sorry. Just zoned out."

The trainer's eyes narrowed. "Are you okay? You look tired."

She sighed. "I was up late last night. Some asshole spray-painted my car. My next-door neighbor scared him off when he got home from work around one a.m."

"Oh, my God!" Tori's eyes widened in shock. "Why would someone do that? Was it kids?"

"I don't know why they did it, and, no, Tuff thinks it was an adult."

"Tuff? You mean Jason Tanner?"

Chet cocked her head to the side. "You know him?"

"Mm-hmm. I've met him a few times at the Trident

compound. Kat told me he was your new neighbor. He's a nice guy—cute too. I love his tattoos."

Rolling her eyes, she teasingly chastised her friend. "You have not one but two hot-as-hell fiancés, you don't need to be ogling any other guys."

It was true. Tori had fallen in love with two men, who both loved her and each other as well. Theirs was a true ménage relationship, but as long as everything was consensual, the threesome didn't bother Chet at all. In fact, she admired Tori for having the courage to follow her heart and be in a relationship that was shunned by many, even in today's society. Chet had met Mitch Sawyer and Tyler Ellis several times, and not only were they nice, but they were hunks too. Tori had hit the jackpot with those two.

"As long as I don't touch, I'm allowed to ogle." She chuckled. "As long as I don't ogle in front of Mitch and Ty, of course." She gestured to the beagle mix and golden doodle lying beside Chet's feet. "Now, let's put these two through their paces and see if we can't start them on the way to their forever homes."

BLACKHAWK SECURITY

CHAPTER SEVEN

Pulling her rented SUV into the driveway, a smile spread across Chet's face. Aside from having to drop her vehicle off at a body shop this morning and secure a rental, it'd been a good day. Pepper and Diego had both been accepted into the PTSD canine program, Meat had been a very good boy throughout the day, and Tuff was at her front door. He was standing on a small ladder, installing a security camera, while wearing cargo shorts, sneakers, and nothing more. Sweat glistened across his exposed skin. His bare back was as colorfully decorated as his arms, with the main focus being a large, stunning image of the Archangel Gabriel, if Chet wasn't mistaken. She stared at him through her windshield as his muscles rippled with the slightest movement. Damn, the man was gorgeous. If she didn't get ahold of herself, she'd be drooling all over like Meat was doing in the backseat.

Her leering was interrupted when her cell phone rang. Pulling it from the outside pocket of her tactical bag, which stored much of what she needed while on duty, she glanced at the screen. *Mom*. Chet cheerfully answered the call. "Hi, Mom!"

"Hi, sweetie. Are you busy?"

She wasn't about to tell her mother that she'd interrupted Chet leering at her hot next-door neighbor. "Not at all. I just got home. What's up?"

"I wanted to ask you something. I talked to Aunt Rita last night, and her tenants decided not to renew their lease, so she asked if I'd be interested in renting the apartment in her house."

That ripped the last of Chet's attention away from Tuff. "What? I thought you didn't want to leave Chicago."

Her mom sighed. "Your *father* didn't want to leave Chicago. I'd tried to talk him into moving a few times after you all were out on your own, but you know he never liked change. So we stayed here. Now that he's gone . . . there are too many memories here, happy and sad. It's also a big house for just me. I think it's time for me to sell it and wanted your opinion."

"If you're calling to ask my permission, Mom, it's not necessary."

Although Chet was surprised at the sudden topic of her mom wanting to move, she worried about the older woman being alone in the big house. Chet was the middle child out of three and the only one who'd moved from the Humboldt Park neighborhood on the west side of Chicago. Her father had died almost two years ago after a six-month battle with cancer. At first, Chet hated the fact her dad hadn't been around to walk her down the aisle eight months later, but she was glad he hadn't seen her marriage turn into a disaster. Chet's mother knew why she'd filed for divorce, though. The first words out of Mariana Suarez's mouth, after she'd asked if Chet was okay, was, "I knew I didn't like that *cabrón*."

"I would love for you to move to Venice with Aunt Rita."

It was only an hour south of Tampa, and Chet knew the two women would have no trouble living beside each other. They'd been childhood best friends who'd become sisters-in-law when Mariana fell in love with Rita's older brother and married him in her early twenties. Aunt Rita and her late husband had moved to Florida about fifteen years ago when his job transferred him, but the two women still talked to each other practically every day. "What did Lorenzo and Mia say about it?"

"Your brother is fine with it. You know he wants to move down to Florida once he gets his twenty years in for his police department pension. As for your sister . . ." When her mother paused like that, it was usually accompanied by an eye roll. "Well, you know her. She doesn't want me to move."

"That's because she'll lose her free babysitter." Although Chet loved her younger sister, Mia was a tad selfish at times —and that was putting it mildly. "Too bad. Sophie is almost twelve—she'll be old enough soon to watch her two brothers after school until Mia gets home." Her sister was a legal secretary, while her husband owned a landscape business that operated mostly in the suburbs.

"That's what I said too. Anyway, I think I'm going to fly down to see Rita next month for a week before I make my final decision. Will it be okay if I stay with you for a few days?"

"Of course, Mom! I'd love to see you. Just let me know which days you'll be here, and I'll take them off. I have plenty of vacation days saved up, so it's not a problem."

"Wonderful. I'm looking forward to seeing your new place."

"I can't wait to see you! Oh, I'm so excited!" While she did miss her mother, Florida was Chet's home. She'd fallen in love with the Gulf Coast on a trip to visit a friend who'd moved there ten years ago. The following year, Chet had packed up and moved south. Her first job had been in a veterinarian's office. Six months later, she'd started training as an animal control officer and had worked for the county ever since.

Behind her, Meat barked once, and Chet looked up to see Tuff descending the stairs, grinning at her. He had the most adorable dimples, which made her stomach do flip-flops. Unfortunately, he'd put his T-shirt back on. Her mother was wrapping up the conversation, so Chet held up a finger to let Tuff know she was almost done with the call. He nodded and stopped at the front of the SUV.

"I love you too, Mom. Call me when you know what dates you'll be here . . . Okay, talk to you soon. Bye."

Chet turned off the engine and climbed out of the vehicle. "Sorry about that. That was my mom."

"No worries," he responded as Chet opened the rear door and grabbed Meat's leash before letting him jump out. "Hey, Meatball. How're ya doing, boy?" Although he was still hesitant to approach the man, the dog did a little happy dance, his tail wagging furiously as he let out a woof. Tuff chuckled at him. "Glad to hear it." He fell in step with Chet, on the opposite side from Meat, as she started for the stairs. "How'd the training tryouts go?"

She'd been surprised when she'd answered her phone earlier in the day to find Tuff on the other end of the call. Apparently, when she'd rattled off her phone number to the cops last night, he'd jotted it down too—not that she really minded after all he'd done and was still doing for her. The reason he'd called had been to ask her permission to use the spare key he had for her unit, which he used for the minor repairs he did for his cousin. She'd known about that when she'd signed the lease and had been assured Tuff wouldn't go into her place without express consent. Clearly, he'd kept his word. After she'd given him the okay to enter her half of the duplex to install the wiring for the cameras he was mounting above her front and back doors, he'd asked about her day, and they'd chatted for a bit. When she'd disconnected the call, she'd been stunned to see they'd chatted for over twenty minutes. She usually wasn't a big talker on the phone, preferring face-to-face conversation, but something about talking to Tuff made the time fly by.

"Good. Both Pepper and Diego are perfect for the program."

"That's great." When they reached the top of the stairs, Tuff opened her still unlocked door for her and Meat, then stepped into the foyer after them. There were a few boxes and his large toolbox sitting on the floor.

Chet unhooked Meat's leash and followed the dog as he headed for his water bowl in the kitchen. She glanced over her shoulder. "By the way, I didn't know you knew Tori Freyja."

"Tori? Oh, Mitch and Ty's fiancée." He chuckled. "That still sounds so weird to say, but hey, if they're happy as a threesome, more power to them. Anyway, yeah, I've met her a few times at the Trident compound. Was it her charity you brought the dogs to?"

"Yup. She's helped place dozens of dogs with veterans."

When she opened the refrigerator and silently offered him a beer, he nodded. "Thanks." He accepted the bottle from her and twisted the top off. "Yeah, one of Trident's mechanics is a vet who has a dog she trained. I didn't know him before that, but from what Russ says, Jagger gave him his life back. He'd been living on the streets, worried he'd hurt someone while having a flashback. That fear had prevented him from trying to find a job and somewhere to live."

Chet opened her beer and took a sip. "And that's exactly why I love helping Tori find dogs to train and place. We did a fundraiser last year for Healing Heroes, and many of the veterans and their service dogs came. It was so great to see all the vets doing something so simple as walking through a park, knowing they might not have been able to without their companion."

"Definitely a great cause."

Silence fell between them for a moment, then both began talking simultaneously.

"Would you like—"

"Why don't I show you—"

A broad grin spread across Tuff's face. "You first."

Her cheeks burned. Her question had popped into her head, and she'd started to blurt it out before she could think twice about it, but now she was nervous. Taking a deep breath, she forged ahead. "I wanted to know if you'd like to have dinner with me tonight. It's—um—it's the least I could do after all you've done for me—last night, today, and with Meat."

Chet's stomach dropped when he didn't answer immediately, instead taking a deep breath and letting it out slowly. "I would love to have dinner with you, but I'm not sure it's a good idea."

Her gaze hit the floor, and she pivoted away, embarrassment and disappointment coursing through her. "That's okay ... I understand."

After setting his beer on the counter, Tuff gently grasped her upper arm and turned her back around to face him. He tilted her chin up until their eyes met. "I don't think you *do* understand, Chet. Far from it. I'm attracted to you and growing more so every day. I'm also getting the feeling you're attracted to me too. But you deserve someone who can give you a lot more than I can."

When she opened her mouth to refute him, he shook his head and continued. "I haven't had the greatest track record with relationships—I'm not exactly boyfriend material. My job takes me away a lot, and when I come back from some assignments, I can be a bear with a thorn in its paw for a few days. I see shit no human should see. I can give you friendship—hell, I can even give you sex—but that's all it would ever be, and you deserve more than that. Especially after dealing with your crappy ex-husband. I'm afraid if we take this thing between us past the friendship level, it'll end in disaster, and that'll make living next to each other a nightmare."

While she was sure his speech had been meant to dissuade her, it'd done the opposite. She fell for the man a little more in those few moments. He cared about her enough not to want to hurt her and to make her understand why he was turning her down. But his resolve had reminded her of all the reasons why it wasn't a good idea to get involved with him.

Making a decision, Chet straightened her back. "You're a really nice guy, Tuff. I hope someday you find someone who can make you happy enough to stay with her, but in the meantime, you have to eat, right?"

His playful grin returned as he dipped his chin down and then up once. "Right."

"Good. Then I'm offering my new friend some pasta primavera for dinner to thank him for all he's done for me. There's nothing wrong with that, right?"

"Right," he repeated. He squeezed her shoulders, then released her and stepped back. She immediately missed the warmth of his touch. "In that case, I'd be honored to have dinner with you."

BLACKHAWK SECURITY

CHAPTER EIGHT

Tuff would kick himself in the ass if he could for two completely different reasons. First, for putting that embarrassment and hurt in Chet's eyes when he'd first said he didn't think it was a good idea to have dinner with her. And, second, for giving in and accepting her invitation, despite all those reasons he'd stated not to. At least he was getting a delicious meal out of it and some good company. Now, if he could leave her house without kissing her again, he'd be all set.

After taking a fast shower in his unit and then showing her where the new cameras were, inside and out, he'd helped Chet chop the vegetables for the pasta and tried to ignore how good it felt doing something mundane with her. He'd never had such a feeling of domesticity come over him while hanging out with a woman. Hell, he couldn't even remember the last time he'd cooked a meal with a woman. Usually, he took his dates out to eat. But then again, this wasn't a date.

Taking a sip of his second beer, he washed down the last bite of his meal. "That was amazing. Do you cook a lot?"

Chet shrugged as she used her fork to push the food

around on her plate. She hadn't eaten much and still seemed a little out of sorts. Tuff suspected he was the cause of both. At least he didn't have to drag a conversation out of her. "A little. Most of the time, I try to make stuff I can freeze in single servings, so I just have to reheat them. Sometimes it's not worth cooking for just one person."

"I hear you. I eat takeout far too much sometimes because I'm not in the mood to cook after a long day. Maybe I'll take your idea and make extra to freeze." *Or maybe I can cook a meal for both of us, followed by a roll in the sack. Shut up, Evil Tuff. Fuck you, goody-two-shoes Tuff!*

Ugh, there were times his inner, juvenile angel and devil had some knock-down, drag-out fights, and he didn't need that right now. He had to stay focused, or he'd do something he'd regret. Like, kiss Chet again. Yeah, he kept repeating to himself what a bad idea that was, but his mouth and cock weren't on the same wavelength as his mind.

Tuff was about to say something else but froze instead. Chet stared at his shocked expression. "What's wrong?"

"Slowly and very quietly, look under the table."

Her brow furrowed, but she did as instructed. When she lifted her head again, there was a huge grin on her face and delight in her eyes. "Looks like you won him over."

Leaning back, Tuff peered down at his feet. He couldn't see them, though, because Meat had decided to use them as a pillow. His massive head rested on one, while an oversized paw covered the other. "Guess so. The only problem is I can't move now." The dog let out a loud snore, and Tuff chuckled. "Yup. I'm not going anywhere for a while. I don't have the heart to wake him."

Easing to her feet so she didn't disturb the dog, Chet cleared the dishes from the table. "No problem. How about a cup of coffee or cappuccino?"

"Mmm. Cappuccino sounds good. I wish I could help you clean up."

"No worries. It's only one extra place setting. Besides, I'm glad Meat feels comfortable enough to cuddle up to you."

As she bent over to put things in the dishwasher or fridge, Tuff couldn't keep his gaze off her ass. He'd been semi-hard for her since he'd followed her up the steps earlier and watched that derrière sway back and forth. Now, he was growing even harder. Damn it! How the hell was he going to remain just friends with Chet if he couldn't stop thinking about her in his bed? Under him. Over him. Screaming his name at the top of her lungs as she shattered for him.

He cleared his suddenly dry throat and took another swig of beer. "So . . . um . . . you mentioned earlier your mom was coming to visit next month. From where?"

Chet glanced over her shoulder at him before going back to cleaning the sauté pan she'd cooked in. "She still lives in the home I grew up in on the west side of Chicago. It's not huge, but she has no use for the two empty bedrooms and finished basement anymore. My Aunt Rita has a house with an attached apartment down in Venice, and the tenants decided to move out, so she invited my mom to take it. Aunt Rita is my dad's sister, and she and Mom have been best friends since they were young. Now that Dad's gone, I think it will do them both good to live next to each other, and I'll love having my mom close again."

When she stopped talking, Tuff said, "Tell me more about your family."

For the next two hours, while they drank cappuccinos and Meat sawed wood under the table, Tuff learned so much more than just about Chet's family. Before and during dinner, they'd kept the conversation light but then slowly progressed into deeper topics. That's when Tuff realized he was in so much trouble. She fascinated him in a way no other woman had. Of course, he wanted her in his bed—most heterosexual males would—but he also enjoyed just being in her company. She was passionate about her family, her job, the animals she rescued and those she couldn't save, and every other subject that came up. She challenged him to debates and really listened to his point of view before presenting her own. Then she agreed to disagree without getting all pissed off like some other women he'd dated. Not that he and Chet were dating, he reminded himself again, but all those reasons he'd spouted off earlier were being pushed to the back of his mind. What he really wanted to do was kiss the ever-loving hell out of her and see where they went from there.

When Meat snorted himself awake, the dog rolled to his feet and ambled over to his water dish. Once he was done drinking, Chet got to her feet and let him out the backdoor to do his business in her half of the fenced-in yard. As much as he wanted to stay, Tuff took that as his cue to leave.

"I think I should get going. You had a long day." Pushing back from the table, he stood, then picked up both empty coffee cups and put them in the dishwasher for her. "Thanks for dinner, Chet."

She smiled and followed as he walked toward the foyer. "You're welcome. It was nice to have the company for a change."

"That it was." He glanced around to make sure he'd grabbed all his tools and the empty boxes when he'd packed up and put them in his unit earlier. Still hesitant to leave, he stuffed his hands in the pockets of the jeans he'd put on after his shower. "I set the motion sensor lights to pick up movement at a further distance. They'll go off if anyone walks within seventy-five feet of the front and sides of the house and one-hundred feet in the backyard. Any further than the seventy-five out front, they'd pick up anyone driving or walking by and going on and off all night."

"Great. Thanks."

Tuff inhaled deeply, then exhaled. "I better go. Deadbolt the doors and keep your gun close. If I hear Meat go ballistic, I'll be knocking on your door to make sure you're all right."

"Yes, Dad," she teased with an eye roll.

He chuckled. "Yeah, the last thing I want you calling me is 'Dad.' Listen, I know you can defend yourself, and Meat won't let anyone near you, but that doesn't mean I won't worry about your safety. I care about you."

Her cheeks pinkened. "Thanks. I care about you too."

Tuff opened his mouth and then closed it again before he said something incredibly stupid. Mentally, he shook his head, then grabbed the doorknob. "Good night, Chet."

"Good night, Tuff."

"Don't give me those sad eyes, Meat. You know you have to stay in the kennel while I'm on duty." Chet wasn't comfortable leaving him alone at her place yet, even though it wouldn't be a problem for her to stop in once or twice during the day. She didn't think he was ready to be alone yet, and he needed to be supervised if men or other dogs were around. He seemed to be doing okay with dogs his own size, but smaller ones made him nervous. Chet would be horrified if something triggered him to attack a smaller dog or a person. The staff at the county shelter was top-notch and would care for and play with him during the day, along with all the other animals in their charge who were being fostered or waiting for forever homes. Meat had his own run with a flap-covered door for him to go inside or out.

"And don't worry. Sherri will play ball with you in a little bit." The woman was one of the best kennel workers they had there, and she was great with the bigger dogs, exerting her dominance over them but with tenderness. Meat loved playing fetch with her.

"Chet, can you come into the office for a minute?"

She turned toward the door at the end of the row of kennels, many filled with barking dogs. The door was ajar, and Des Edkins had stuck his head around the jamb. The man looked pale and worried.

With one last glance at the lock on Meat's kennel to ensure it was secure, she started walking toward the door. "Yeah, sure. What's wrong?"

"In my office."

Chet's eyes narrowed as her boss disappeared into the hallway. Moments later, she entered his office and was surprised to see two Tampa P.D. plainclothes detectives standing there—their sidearms and shields attached to their belts gave them away.

Des gestured for her to take one of the seats in front of his desk while he sat behind it. "Detectives Isaac Webb and Sonja Lovett, this is Officer Concetta Suarez." The two nodded hello to her, but their blank expressions worried her. Neither spoke but allowed Des to continue. "Chet, I don't know how to break this to you gently, but Terry Spender and his wife were killed late last night."

"What? Oh, my God, what happened?" She was beyond being in shock. When Chet had started at Animal Control, Terry had been her training officer. They'd hit it off and become good friends, despite the man being twenty-three years her senior. Chet had attended his wedding seven months before he and his wife, Megan, had attended hers. It'd been a second marriage for Terry, having lost his first wife to a sudden brain aneurysm ten years earlier. He'd even become a grandfather a few months back.

Des and the detectives spent the next few minutes filling her in and asking some questions. It'd been a drive-by shooting when the couple had arrived home from a late night of dinner and dancing with a few friends. There were no witnesses—possibly a case of mistaken identity, a robbery gone wrong, or some sort of a road-rage incident where the suspect, or suspects, had followed them home before opening fire as they exited their vehicle. Megan had been killed instantly, while Terry had been pronounced dead at the ER after the medics and hospital staff had done everything they could to save him.

Uncontrollable tears rolled down Chet's cheeks as she grieved for her friend and mentor and his wife while the detectives asked her several questions. *Was either of them having trouble with anyone? Do you know if they were experiencing financial or marital trouble? Were either of them estranged from their children? Was there any friction between the two combined families? Can you think of anyone who could have done this? Do you know if either one of them had a gambling, drinking, or drug problem? Do you know if Terry had any incidents on the job that may have followed him into his private life?*

Her response to all was an emphatic "no." Well, except for that last one. More than once, every Animal Control Officer for Hillsborough County had been threatened after they'd taken abused and neglected animals from their cruel owners. Some had even shown up at the shelter, demanding the animals be returned to them, and TPD officers had needed to respond and intervene.

After the detectives thanked her and said she could leave, before requesting Des bring in another employee to interview, her boss followed Chet out into the currently empty hallway. He pulled her into a comforting hug. "I'm so sorry, Chet. I know how close you and Terry were. I want you to take the rest of the day off and tomorrow, too, if needed."

When she shook her head, he continued. "That's not a request—it's an order. I'll tell almost everyone that while keeping just a skeleton crew here. I'll stay too. The cops can handle most animal calls for the day. I'll contact the courts and see if anything on the schedules can be postponed."

Chet wiped her tears and took a step back. "I don't have any court cases today."

"Good. Then take Meat home with you. If you need to talk, I'm here, okay?"

"Okay." She glanced to the right and then the left, suddenly unsure of where she was and what she needed to do. She expected to see Terry strolling in through the door at the end of the hall that led to the parking lot, but he'd never do that again. Taking a deep breath, she nodded at Des. "Okay. I'll get Meat. You'll call if you hear anything new?"

"I promise. Drive safely."

Chet cringed inwardly. "Drive safely" was something Terry said to her almost every time they parted. The man had reminded her so much of her own father, and she would miss him just as much.

CHAPTER NINE

Squatting in the cool shade of his garage, Tuff wiped down his motorcycle with a clean rag after he changed the oil. It was a sweet 1945 Indian Chief Civilian Model he'd lovingly restored to its original beauty after snagging it at an auction a few years ago. After getting it purring like a lion cub, he'd had a former SEAL teammate of the Trident Security Alpha Team, Curt Bannerman, design and apply the MIA-tribute paint job. The guy had been over the moon to work on the vintage bike since they didn't come around too often. Tuff had wanted to honor all the men and women who'd fought for their country and gone missing in action. The US was doing its best to bring them all home, but with more than 80,000 American service members whose bodies have been unaccounted for since the start of the twentieth century, many MIAs would never be found. Thousands were lost in the waters surrounding islands involved in war or conflict, such as Hawaii, the Solomon Islands, the Korean Peninsula, and the Philippines. More went missing in the middle of the vast oceans of the world when either their planes or ships had gone down. Then there were those who'd disappeared and presumably died in foreign countries decades ago. At least some of those were slowly being discovered each year. Once found, their remains were returned to the US, where they were properly buried with full military honors.

Behind Tuff stood the 1994 Harley-Davidson Heritage Softail he also owned, which had required a little tinkering and TLC, too, when he'd first gotten it. For that paint job, he'd asked Bannerman to pay tribute to men and women in the armed forces who'd lost their lives during the wars in Afghanistan and Iraq, some of whom he'd known personally.

Tuff had the morning off since the detail he and three teammates were assigned to didn't start until 3:00 p.m. That had left too much time for his mind to wander to last night. It had taken everything in him not to lean in and kiss Chet goodnight before he left. Each minute he spent in her lovely presence was another spot where she'd been imprinted on his heart. Despite all his reasons for telling her it was best they remain just friends, he wanted her more than any other woman he'd ever met. He tried convincing himself he *shouldn't* want her—it was in everybody's best interest that he didn't—but that made him crave her even more.

"Hey, Tuff!"

"Hi, Tuff!"

He glanced up and waved at two of the neighborhood boys riding their bikes past his driveway. With towels around their necks and board shorts and T-shirts on, it was a safe bet the thirteen-year-olds were heading to their friend's house two blocks away to spend the day in his pool. They alternated hanging out at each other's houses, and sometimes Tuff joined them and a few of the older kids in the middle of the cul-de-sac to throw a baseball or football around or shoot some hoops at the backboard that stood at the end of one of the driveways.

Grabbing a nearby water bottle, he took a long, cool drink. The temperature was already in the low nineties, and it was barely 9:30 in the morning. Having done numerous tours in deserts on the other side of the world, the heat and humidity of Florida didn't bother Tuff until it was well over one hundred degrees, which it was forecast to reach tomorrow. Thank God for air conditioning.

Ten minutes later, he'd just finished putting everything back where it belonged and was surprised to see Chet's department-issued SUV pull into the driveway. Giving his hands a final wipe of the towel, he strolled out to see her. When she climbed out of the vehicle, still in her uniform, and he saw her swollen, red eyes and tear-stained face, he threw the towel to the ground and rushed to her side. "Chet, what's wrong? Are you okay?"

Rapidly shaking her head and pursing her lips, she opened the rear door and grabbed the end of Meat's leash. "No—no, I'm not. I—"

Her words were cut off by a heart wrenching sob, and Tuff stepped around the dog, who'd jumped to the ground, and pulled Chet into an embrace. It was then she completely lost it, bawling and trembling in his arms. Her hands went behind his back and clutched his sweaty T-shirt. At their feet, Meat whined and leaned against his mistress. Tuff held Chet tightly, stroking her hair. "Sh. Easy, baby. I've got you . . . I've got you."

After a few moments, Chet tried to step back, but Tuff wouldn't let her. Tucking her under one arm, he shut the SUV's rear door, then walked her and Meat to the stairs and up to her front door, which he unlocked with his spare key. Once inside, he gently pushed her to sit on the couch. "Stay there a second. Let me get Meat some water."

Grabbing the dog's bowl in the kitchen, he filled it with water and placed it back on the floor. Panting, Meat padded in and made a beeline for it. Tuff then opened the fridge, snatched a bottle of water he knew Chet kept in there, and brought it out to her. "Drink, and then we'll talk."

After making sure she was hydrating herself, he hurried to the half bath in the hallway and returned with a box of tissues. He took out two and handed them to her before sitting beside her and putting an arm around her shoulders. "What happened, baby?"

Through her tears, she told him about the homicide of her mentor and the man's wife. It was evident she'd been close to the couple, and his heart broke for her. "I-I still can't believe it. Th-they were the nicest people in the world! Why w-would someone do that—that to them?"

He wished he had an answer for her, but he knew all too well that bad things happened to good people and often never made sense to those left behind.

A half-hour later, Chet was all cried out and crashing. Her eyes became heavy as she cuddled into his side, her head resting on his shoulder. Placing one hand under her knees and the other at her back, Tuff stood with her in his arms and strode toward her bedroom. The fact she didn't protest worried him. Setting her in the middle of the queen-sized bed, he removed her work boots and pulled a blanket, which had been folded over the footboard, on top of her. Unable to leave her alone right away, he sat next to her on the bed and ran his hand up and down her arm while Meat lay on the floor nearby.

Sleep hit Chet hard, and once Tuff was certain she was out, he eased himself up and quietly left the room, leaving the door ajar in case she woke up and needed him. Pacing the kitchen, he pulled out his cell phone and dialed the BHS office. When Chase's receptionist answered, he said, "Hi, Shannon, it's Tuff. Is Chase around?"

"Hi, Tuff. He's on a conference call at the moment, but Irv is available. Do you want to talk to him instead?"

"Yeah, thanks."

"No problem. Hang on."

After a few clicks, the deep voice of Blackhawk's Senior Executive Officer came over the line. "Hey, Tuff. What's up?"

He let out a heavy sigh. "Irv, I hate to do this, but is there any way you can swap me out on today's detail?"

"Everything okay?"

There was no mistaking the surprise in the other man's voice, but it was easy to figure out what he was thinking. Tuff couldn't remember the last time he'd asked to be pulled from a detail unless it'd been doctor's orders for an illness or injury. He also had a stockpile of personal and vacation days that he rarely used. If he did, they were always scheduled in advance.

"I'm good, but a friend really needs me."

There was a long pause. "Okay. I'll assign someone else. Is this just for today, or do I have to move things around tomorrow too?"

Meat trotted into the kitchen and sat in front of him, looking up pleadingly. Tuff grinned and shook his head. "I'm not sure yet. Can I get back to you in a bit?"

"Sure. Just make it as soon as possible, so I'm not scrambling at the last minute."

"No problems, and thanks, Irv."

"Yup."

Disconnecting the call, Tuff stared down at the dog, who lifted his front leg. "Don't give me that look or the paw. I know you get fed in the morning and again around five. Just because your momma brought you home doesn't mean it's dinner time, so don't try to con me. But if you promise to watch Chet for a few minutes while I run and shower, then I'll give you a treat. Deal?"

"*Woof.*"

"*Ruhig*—not too loud. Now be good, and I'll be right back."

He left the front door unlocked, knowing the dog wouldn't allow anyone else to enter, before stepping into his own unit. After a fast shower to wash the sweat and grease off his skin, he threw on a clean pair of cargo shorts, a T-shirt with the Blackhawk logo on it, and flip-flops. Next, he grabbed his laptop so he had something to do while Chet slept, and then took out a bone for Meat from the freezer where he'd stored the extras he'd gotten the other day. But before he headed for the door, he returned to his bedroom and retrieved a holstered 9mm from the closet. He had several weapons stashed throughout the house in case of trouble—which in his business was always a possibility. After holstering it and tucking it inside his back waistband, he returned to Chet's place.

Meat growled softly when the front door opened but immediately quieted when he saw Tuff. The big lug's tail thwacked against the hardwood floor in the hallway, just beyond the tiled foyer. "All quiet?"

With his head down, the dog stood and took a few steps toward Tuff, who held the bone up. "*Sitz.*" When the dog sat, Tuff told him he was a good dog using the German words Chet had taught him. "*Braver Hund.*" He gave Meat his reward, and the dog gently took it from him. "There you go—you deserve it. Enjoy."

As the pit bull lay down in the living room to snack on his bone, Tuff sat on the couch. His cell phone rang as he booted up his laptop. Glancing at the screen, he saw it was Blackhawk's main number—probably Irv calling him back. "Hello?"

"Tuff," Chase responded without preamble. "Talk to me."

Knowing he should've expected a follow-up call from the

owner of the security company, Tuff leaned back on the couch. "Hey, Chase. Sorry about the late call out, but a friend of mine lost someone to a homicide last night and just found out about it this morning."

"Friend? Wouldn't happen to be a woman, would it?"

His eyes narrowed. "Yeah, Chet's a woman. She lives in the other half of my duplex."

"Should have known," his boss said with a chuckle. "I'm not letting any of my single guys work with Trident anymore. Those idiots drop like flies over there whenever a woman bats their eyes at them. Must be fucking contagious. Does this have anything to do with the vandalism the other night?"

That thought had crossed Tuff's mind earlier, but he'd quickly dismissed it. He'd mentioned the incident the other night to Irv when he'd gotten the okay to swipe a few extra security cameras from the company stock. Having Chase bring it up again had him scratching his head. "I can't make the connection if it does, but stranger things have happened. Can you find out the details of the homicide for me?"

"What's the victim's name?"

"It was a couple—Terry and Megan Spender. A drive-by as they got out of their car at home late last night."

"Saw that on the news earlier. How does your woman know them?"

Tuff got a funny feeling in his chest at his boss's words that he didn't want to analyze too deeply. *Your woman.* It'd felt good to hear Chet being referred to like that.

"Um, the guy trained her at Animal Control and has been a close friend for the past eight years or so. She was close with both of them." He'd added that last part because he didn't want Chase thinking Chet and Terry had been romantically involved or anything. Hell, Tuff didn't want to think about her being romantically involved with *anyone*. He was so fucking screwed.

"All right. I'll see what I can find out. In the meantime, stay alert, and don't fucking propose."

Before a stunned Tuff could respond to the command said in jest, Chase had disconnected the call. Shaking his head, Tuff tossed the phone onto the couch next to him. While he'd been caught off guard, the thought of asking Chet to marry him didn't sound as scary and ridiculous as it would have a few days ago.

Tuff looked at Meat, who stopped gnawing on the bone and returned the stare while tilting his head. "She's too good for me."

The dog shook his head from side to side, his jowls and ears flopping away. Tuff snorted. "Is that a no, she's not, or are you agreeing with me?"

"*Rowf!*"

"To hell with German. If we're going to have a conversation, I gotta teach you to speak English."

CHAPTER TEN

Chet woke up confused. She was dressed in her uniform, but her shoes were off, and she was lying in her bed. The sun was shining into her bedroom from the west, which meant it was late in the day. She glanced at the bedside clock and was stunned to see it was 5:37 p.m.

Her gut clenched as the horrible morning rushed back to her. She wished it had been nothing more than a bad dream but knew that wasn't true. Terry and Megan were dead. They'd dated for five years, living together for three, before they'd finally tied the knot, and Chet had spent many fun times at their house with their families and friends. Every year, the couple had a huge Fourth of July barbecue and a festive Christmas party the Saturday before the holiday. They would invite friends with nowhere to go on the holidays to join them. There would be many people who were going to miss the gregarious couple.

She remembered driving home in tears and falling into Tuff's arms, bawling hysterically. Yeah, that must have been attractive. Chet was an ugly crier. She vaguely recalled him carrying her to bed. He must have left after she fell asleep, although she couldn't blame him. Many guys didn't know how to deal with a crying woman.

Drawing the blanket off the lower half of her body, Chet rolled over and got to her feet. Her bladder was ready to burst. Once she was done in the bathroom, she changed out of her uniform and into a pair of cotton shorts and a T-shirt, minus her bra. She had marks where it'd dug into her flesh while she'd been sleeping.

Shuffling out of the bedroom, she hoped Meat hadn't had any accidents in the house. While he'd been really good about that since the third day after she'd brought him home, Chet tried to keep him on a schedule of going for a walk every three hours from 7:00 a.m. to 9:00 p.m. She'd shut the bedroom door so he didn't wander at night and also kept the toilet seat cover down so he couldn't sneak a drink from the bowl.

Halfway down the hall, Chet froze. Not only was the smell of something delicious tempting her nose, but she could hear Tuff talking in the kitchen. And from the sound of it, he was conversing with her foster dog.

"So, whatta you think about this new kid the Rays called up from Triple-A, Meatball? His fastball is awesome, but I think his slider needs some work. Not sure if we got the better end of that trade last year or not. Time will tell."

Chet heard Meat make a funny sound, which was like a cross between a groan and him trying to speak. She bit her lip when Tuff responded. "What's that? Oh, yeah, Vickars is definitely in a major hitting slump right now, but Flitch's and Bentley's bats have been hot lately, so they've been saving his ass. Hopefully, Taniguchi comes off the D.L. soon, though—we need him back in center field."

Despite everything that had happened earlier, Chet couldn't help but smile and giggle softly at Tuff's conversation with the big pit bull. Before she could make her presence known, the doorbell rang, and Meat started barking his head off as he ran toward the foyer, his nails clicking loudly on the wood and tile flooring.

"Meat, ruhig," Tuff ordered in a dominant tone. He strode right by Chet without seeing her standing around the corner in the shorter hallway off the longer one that led to the front door, pulling his wallet out of his shorts as he went. "Sitz! Braver Hund. It's just the Chinese food delivery. I'll read your fortune cookie if you don't try to take a bite out of the guy."

Tuff unlocked and cracked open the front door. "Sorry, but I can't open it any further. How much was it?" The response was too muffled for Chet to hear. "Here you go. Thanks." He closed the door and locked it again. "Hmm. You like the smell of Chinese food, don't you . . . hey, you're up. I hope Meat didn't wake you. Sorry about the racket."

Chet grinned at Tuff as he stopped and looked her up and down. The dog rushed over to her and demanded some attention, so she scratched his ears. "No worries. I was already wide awake before the doorbell rang. I didn't know you were still here."

She followed him into the kitchen, where he set down two bags of food on the table. The aroma of whatever he'd ordered, combined with a hot apple pie cooling on the stove, made her stomach growl. Tuff grinned, clearly having heard she was hungry. "I only left to shower and change. I brought my laptop over to do some work and stuff. Meat and I have been having a grand old time, haven't we, boy?"

"*Rowf!*"

Taking Chet by the shoulders, Tuff steered her into a seat. "Relax, and I'll get the plates and utensils. Do you want water, soda, beer, wine, or something I didn't notice you have?"

"Um, I can get it." She started to rise but stopped when he

glared at her. When she slowly sat back down, his smile returned, giving her a warm, fuzzy feeling. "A root beer, please. Thank you."

"You're welcome. If you want to help, you can start pulling out the containers and see what you're in the mood to eat." He set an empty plate in front of her along with a knife and fork, then put another place setting across from her. "I found the apple pie in your freezer—I hope you don't mind that I heated it up."

"I don't mind at all. Thanks for doing all this."

"My pleasure."

As he gathered their sodas and glasses filled with ice, Chet checked out each container as she pulled them out of the full paper bags. "Who are we feeding, an army? Shrimp rolls, hot and sour soup, steamed dumplings, General Tso's chicken, beef lo mein, moo shu pork, and shrimp with broccoli. These are all my favorites. How did you know?"

He sat down, grinning. "Meat told me." When she rolled her eyes, he chuckled. "I found a few menus in your takeout box on the counter—that's cute, by the way. Anyway, I flipped through them and saw what was circled from previous orders."

"I didn't realize I had so many duplicates in there. Obviously, I have to clean the box out." It was a decorated, wooden box she'd found in Home Goods, with "Takeout Menus" in script across the top. She stored the ones from her favorite local places that delivered. The box got the menus off the counter, table, and refrigerator and out of her junk drawer and into one cute, neat place.

They loaded their plates, swapping the containers with each other until they both had a little bit of everything. After taking a few mouthfuls to quiet her hungry stomach, she sipped her soda. It was comforting to have Tuff with her tonight. In between bites, he asked her questions, keeping them light and off the subject of the deaths of her friends. He even managed to draw a few chuckles from her by telling her stories from his Army bootcamp days.

After they had their fill, Tuff set about clearing the table and putting the leftovers in the refrigerator. Again, he wouldn't let her help. As she watched him load the dishwasher, a thought crossed her mind. "Weren't you supposed to work tonight?"

"Mm-hmm." He grabbed a sponge from the sink and ran it under the water. "I called and asked my boss to have someone cover for me on the detail."

Her eyes narrowed. "Why?"

Turning to face her, Tuff held her confused gaze with an intense one. "Because I couldn't leave you here alone after finding out two of your friends were killed. I was worried about you, Chet, and wanted to be here in case you needed me."

Silence filled the air as his words swirled around in her mind. He'd called into work only a few hours before he had to be there and took the time off because he was worried about her? Because he wanted to be there if she needed him?

"Oh, hey, baby. I didn't mean to make you start crying again."

Chet could barely see him because of her tears as he crossed the room and rounded the table. As he'd done earlier, he put a hand under her knees and the other around her back before lifting her. Again, he took her seat and set her on his lap. She wrapped her arms around his neck and cried into his hard chest as he stroked her back and murmured words meant to soothe her. As he usually did when she was out of sorts, Meat sat at her feet, whining and nuzzling her side. Tuff was the one to pet the dog's big head. "It's okay, boy. Your momma's going to be fine."

A hiccup, followed by a chuckle, escaped Chet as she

wiped her eyes and cheeks with one hand. It was so adorable how Tuff talked to Meat like he was a little kid who understood everything the man was saying, and it broke through her crying jag. Tuff reached past her, snagged her napkin from the table, and handed it to her. She wiped her eyes again and blew her nose, too late thinking it was not the most attractive thing to do while sitting on a man's lap. A man's muscular lap. A man's warm, muscular lap, with something poking her in the hip. *Oh, boy.*

She lifted her gaze to his and saw desire in his eyes. He licked his lips but didn't make any other movement. Chet wanted those lips on hers. And not for a brief kiss. She wanted to devour him and have him do the same to her. All thoughts of their dinner and the day from hell fled her mind. Her eyelids dropped as she stared at his mouth. Throwing caution to the wind, Chet leaned forward and brushed her lips against Tuff's. He froze beneath her, but she decided she was going all in. She shifted on his lap to get a better angle on his mouth.

His hand dove into her hair and gripped the strands, holding her in place. He pulled back only an inch or two, his gaze scanning her face. "I'm hanging on by a thread here, sweetheart. I don't want to take advantage of you being so upset."

"You won't be. Please, Tuff." Her voice was just above a whisper as she trailed her knuckles across his cheek. "I want you, Jason. No regrets. No demands for promises neither of us can keep. Just live in the moment. I need you to remind me I'm still alive even though I'm dying inside."

CHAPTER ELEVEN

Tuff had been able to fight his urges right up until the moment Chet had called him by his given name and pleaded with him to make her feel alive. He swallowed hard, his mind at war with his body, a war it was going to lose. His lust, combined with the desperation in her eyes, was his final undoing. His hand tightened in her hair as he slammed his mouth down on hers. He had to find that fine line between giving her what she needed without losing his barely-there control. As much as he wanted to carry her to the bedroom and not come back out until they were both sated beyond their wildest dreams, this wasn't about him. It was all about giving Chet the comfort she'd begged him for.

Her lips parted for him, and he slipped his tongue between them, tasting the spicy tang of the General Tao's chicken she'd been eating. She squirmed in his lap, causing his dick to harden more than it'd already been. He'd tried to ignore how her lush ass felt being that close to his cock after he'd set her down on his lap, but the fucker had other plans.

Lifting her, he maneuvered her legs until she was straddling his own. Pulling on her hair, he exposed her neck and feasted on it. Nibbling, sucking, and licking every inch he could reach. His other hand went under the hem of her T-shirt, seeking her breast that he'd already figured out was bare. He'd almost swallowed his tongue earlier when he'd first seen her standing in the hallway, wearing the thin T-shirt. While not sagging, her breasts didn't look as restrained as they normally did. When she moved, they'd swayed just enough to make his mouth water.

Before his hand could reach its destination, Chet reached down and grabbed the front of her shirt. Pulling it up, she forced Tuff's mouth from her skin, so she could completely remove it. He stared at her chest. Damn, those dusky, rose-colored nipples were more beautiful than he'd imagined in his dreams. Cupping one lush orb in his hands, he leaned forward and dragged his tongue over the peaked tip.

Chet moaned and arched her back, bringing his delicious treat closer to his mouth. He sucked on it as her fingers threaded into his short hair, holding him to her. She was so gorgeous, so responsive, Tuff had no idea how he would be able to keep his hands off her after this. Friends with benefits. That's all she'd asked for. Well, not in those exact words. *No regrets. No demands for promises neither of us can keep. Just live in the moment.* He could do that, he'd done it many times before, but for the first time in his life, Tuff wanted more than that—and the woman he was with didn't.

Beside the chair, Meat lay down. Tuff had forgotten the big mutt was there, and it suddenly felt weird to be sucking on Chet's tit with a canine audience. His hands trailed down to her ass, and then he stood. When she squeaked in surprise, he said, "Wrap your legs around me, baby."

When she did as instructed, he carried her to her bedroom and kicked the door shut behind them. Meat could be heard flopping down on the floor on the other side of it. *Sorry, buddy.*

Setting Chet down on the bed, Tuff curled his fingers under the waistband of her sweatpants. He lifted his gaze to hers. "If you want me to stop, Chet, tell me now."

She shook her head. "Don't stop. Please, don't."

Damn, he loved to hear her beg. Tuff dragged her pants and underwear down her legs, then tossed them aside. His heart pounded in his chest as he stared down at her. "You're beautiful, baby. So fucking beautiful."

A blush spread across her chest and face. Her eyes, filled with evident embarrassment, shifted to the side, and that just wouldn't do. Tuff dropped to his knees, next to the bed, between her legs that hung over the side. "Look at me, Concetta." He waited a moment until her gaze returned to his. "You. Are. Beautiful. Don't ever doubt that, bomboncita. And I bet you're even more beautiful when you orgasm—I can't wait to find out for myself."

He leaned down and kissed the inside of one thigh and then the other before his gaze found her face again. "How long has it been for you, sweetheart? I don't want to hurt you."

She licked her lips, and a shiver coursed through her. "Over a year, not including . . . well, you know."

The corners of his mouth ticked upward. "Not including getting yourself off?"

The red on her cheeks deepened as she nodded.

"Damn, that conjures up all sorts of sexy images in my brain." He kissed the soft skin just above her mound. She wasn't bare but neatly trimmed. "I'd love to watch you do that sometime. Do you use a vibrator or just your hand?"

Her gaze flitted to her nightstand, but she didn't verbalize an answer. That was okay, though, because he was now ninety-five percent sure there was a vibrator named Bob or Buzz or some silly name like that tucked away in the drawer. They'd play with it some other time—and there would be another time, he was sure of it. But tonight, it would just be Tuff and Chet.

Pushing against her inner thighs, Tuff spread her wide. Her pussy was already glistening, her labia nicely swollen. He ran the back of his forefinger over her folds, causing her to squirm.

"Please, Tuff."

"Mmm. Don't worry, baby. Relief is coming." Bending down, he rasped his tongue up her slit, reveling in her taste. She bucked her pelvis and cried out. Her hands fisted the blanket that had covered her body earlier as she napped. Trapping her hips under the weight of his arm draped across them, he gave her sweet pussy the utmost attention. His cock throbbed in his shorts, wanting to burst from its confinement and sink into Chet's core, but Tuff ignored it. Any satisfaction he got tonight would be by his own hand. He could give Chet what she needed, but he'd be an asshole if he took advantage of her that way. When he finally took her, she'd be in the right mindset. He was still afraid she'd regret this in the morning, but, God help him, he couldn't stop now.

Tucking his hands under her ass cheeks, he lifted her to give himself better access. His stiffened tongue tunneled its way inside her, making her gasp, moan, and beg. "Oh! Yes! More! Oh, God! More!"

Tuff moved upward and found her exposed clit. He teased the little pearl, flicking his tongue over it before sucking on it. He lowered her ass back down onto the bed so he could use his fingers to fuck her until she came for him. He eased two of them into her core. She was beyond drenched. Her hips undulated as he drove her higher and higher. Her moans became louder. Tuff's cock threatened to explode just from the sounds of Chet chasing her climax. She was killing him.

He curled his fingers and found the bumpy, little patch of tissue that would help him send her into oblivion.

"Oh, my God! Yesssssssss!"

Her walls quivered, then clenched around his fingers, almost crushing them. Her hips bucked, and her legs shook as the waves of pleasure crashed over her. Using his hands and mouth, Tuff drew out her release as long as he could until he felt her orgasm wane.

Gasping for air, Chet sagged into the mattress. Tuff removed his fingers and licked them. Through heavy eyelids, she stared at him, a sexy smile spreading across her face. "That mouth of yours is very talented."

He grinned as he stood and shifted his hips before climbing onto the bed next to her. He put his talented mouth to good use again, kissing her lazily. Chet stretched and rolled toward him onto her side. Her hand worked its way down his chest and over his abdomen, but he grabbed her wrist before it went any further. Pulling her head back, Chet's confused gaze searched his face. Before she could ask him anything, he brought her hand to his mouth and brushed his lips over her knuckles. "Some other time, baby. I know you said you wouldn't regret it in the morning, but I can't take advantage of the situation. I'll cuddle with you, make you come again, and hold you while you sleep. But when I get into that hot pussy of yours, I don't want it to be because you needed an escape. It'll be because you want it more than anything else in the world."

When she opened her mouth to argue with him, he silenced her with his own. He kept the kiss sweet and lazy. When she relaxed, he lifted his head and wrapped his arms around her, tucking her into his chest. "Go to sleep, baby. I'll stay as long as you need me." His hands ran up and down her back and sides in a soothing, continuous path until her breathing evened out.

Tuff's cock wanted relief in the worst way, but holding Chet's sated body in his arms meant more to him than anything. And he didn't know if he'd ever be able to let her go.

CHAPTER TWELVE

As Chet walked from her SUV toward Donovan's Pub, where the repast was being held following Terry and Megan's funeral, her phone vibrated in her pocket. She stopped on the sidewalk and pulled it out, then glanced at the screen. Her heart skipped a beat as she answered the call. "Hi, Tuff."

"Hey, sweetheart. How are you doing?"

Trying to ignore how that term of endearment gave her the warm fuzzies, she sighed and leaned against the stuccoed wall next to the large, plate-glass window of the restaurant. "I'm okay. Just about to walk into Donovan's for the luncheon. The church was packed, but I don't think everyone is coming here. Mostly just the family and close friends."

"I wish I could be there with you. I'm sorry."

While Tuff had attended the wakes with her, both nights, there'd been an emergency detail of some sort, and he and his team had needed to fly somewhere at 10:00 last night, not long after he and Chet had gotten home from the funeral parlor.

"That's okay. Is everything all right? Did you do whatever

it was you had to do?" He hadn't been able to tell her where he'd been going and what he'd be doing there, but Chet wasn't stupid. Through her conversations with Tuff and learning he'd been in Special Forces while in the military, she had to assume he was still doing classified missions for the US, even if it was through the private sector. Men like him never really retired from Special Forces. The government had paid good money for their training, and Uncle Sam would use the men as long as possible.

"Yeah, everything went okay. We should be home tomorrow night, but I don't know if it'll be early enough to see you."

"That's fine. But if you *do* get home early enough, I'd love to see you." Chet grimaced. She didn't know why she'd said that. While Tuff had given her an amazing orgasm the other night, the next morning he seemed to want to continue like it'd never happened. And all Chet could think about was that it *had* happened. No, Tuff wasn't ignoring her or running away from her. In fact, he was more attentive than ever, but he also hadn't given her any indication he wanted to sleep with her again. While there had been hugs of comfort over the past two days, there hadn't been any kisses, heated looks, or seduction. He hadn't mentioned what they'd done, and Chet was too embarrassed to say anything.

She remembered how she'd begged him to help her forget her grief. She'd told him she would have no regrets the next day, and neither of them had to make any promises they knew they couldn't keep. At the time, she thought she'd meant it, but after waking in his warm embrace in the middle of the night, as he snored softly beside her, her feelings had changed. In her heart, she felt more for that man, after only knowing him a few weeks, than she ever had for her ex-husband or any other man. And that scared the hell out of her. Chet didn't want to fall for someone who'd made it clear he couldn't and wouldn't fall for her.

"Well, if your lights are on, I'll knock. If you don't answer, I'll assume you're asleep." He chuckled. "Actually, maybe I shouldn't do that because Meat will make a racket, and that'll wake you up anyway."

Chet couldn't help but smile. She loved when Tuff laughed because she felt it all the way down to her toes.

"By the way, where's the big Meatball?"

"He's at the kennel. Although, he wasn't happy about being left there. He's become quite spoiled lately. He moans every time he knows he's not going with me."

Tuff snorted. "I don't blame him. He's got good taste. If I were him, I'd want to spend the entire day with you too."

She knew she shouldn't read anything into his little joke, but it was hard not to. Glancing up, she noticed a small group of mourners walking toward her. "Listen, my coworkers are coming. Let me get inside with them and grab something to eat."

"Okay. No problem. I was just checking to see how you were doing. I'll talk to you tomorrow night or the next morning."

"Okay, bye."

"Bye."

Disconnecting the call, Chet tucked the phone back in her pocket and pasted a smile on her face, like the ones everyone else from the funeral seemed to be sporting. At least the worst of the day was over, and now they would have some food and drink while sharing some more memories of Terry and Megan.

Two hours later, Chet was sitting with Des and some other coworkers after they'd managed to put some food in their stomachs. As it always did when they were together off the clock, the conversation steered toward work. The sworn-in ACOs would have to plug in the holes in the schedule created by Terry's death until a new person could be hired and fully trained. Des surprised Chet when he told her she would be the recruit's FTO—Field Training Officer.

"What?" Chet asked. "Why me?"

"Because you have more patience than anyone else." The corners of his mouth turned upward, and his voice softened. "And I know you'll do Terry proud."

It'd been a few years since a new animal control officer had been hired. It was a close-knit department, and almost everybody that worked there went beyond the twenty years needed for their pensions just because they enjoyed the job. They loved what they did, took pride in rescuing every animal they could, and liked working among friends. As far as Chet knew, none of the animal control officers planned on retiring anytime soon. Terry probably would've been the next one to put in his papers, but she knew he'd been planning on sticking around for another five years or so.

Chet blushed at the compliment. "Thanks, but shouldn't Matt be the one to train the newbie? He's got seniority now."

Matt McGregor smirked. "And as senior officer, I get to accept or decline a training position, and in this case, I declined, so it falls to you."

She rolled her eyes. "Fine, you don't want it, but what about somebody else? Glenn can do it—he's got patience."

"But it has to be somebody with at least five years' experience," Glenn Fargas responded with a relieved smile. "I only have four and a half so far, so I'm out too. Thank God."

"Fine," Chet repeated before eyeing Des. "Do you know when you'll be hiring somebody?"

He shook his head. "I'm not going to bother looking at the list until Monday. Then I'll bring in the top three people, with the highest scores from the test, for interviews." To be hired as an ACO, a person had to take a civil service exam similar to the one for police officers.

As much as Chet was not looking forward to training somebody new, she tried to look on the positive side. At least it would help keep her mind off of Terry and Megan . . . and Tuff too.

CHAPTER THIRTEEN

Pulling into the driveway, Tuff killed the ignition on his truck. He was exhausted. The mission to rescue a kidnapped businessman in Mexico had been a success, but it'd been hairy there for a bit. A few of his teammates had come home with some bumps and bruises and even a couple of stitches, but those were par for the course for them. As long as everyone was among the walking wounded and not unconscious or worse, then all was good.

On the ride home from the airport, all Tuff had wanted was to climb into his nice, soft bed and sleep for the next twelve hours straight. That was until he saw the light on in Chet's kitchen through the living room window. He knew for a fact she usually didn't leave lights on when she went to bed at night, so had she left it on for him?

It was probably best he didn't find out the answer to that question. During the moments when he'd been allowed to let his mind wander over the past few days, all he'd been able to think about was how good she'd felt in his arms and how she'd shattered under his touch. He got hard every time he thought of his cock nestled against her ass as he'd spooned her while she'd slept the other night. She'd made it crystal clear she hadn't been looking for anything more from him than a way to escape her grief for a little while. With any other woman, he would've been fine with that, but Chet made him wish for things he'd never wanted before.

Grabbing his mission-ready duffel bag to restock it in the morning, he exited the truck. As he climbed the front steps, he had every intention of unlocking his door, closing it behind him, and locking it again, so he wouldn't be tempted to knock on hers. That plan went out the window when Chet's door opened, and she appeared before him with Meat at her side. Tuff did his best to keep his gaze on her face and off her luscious body, but her thin sleep shorts and matching top, clearly sans bra, made that very difficult.

It took a moment for him to realize something wasn't right. She was frowning, worry etched on her face. He immediately stepped closer to her, his protective instincts rising to the surface. "What's wrong, sweetheart?"

She opened the door a little wider. "Can you come in for a minute?"

"Yeah, sure." He brushed past her and gritted his teeth when his bicep made brief contact with the side of her breast.

He set his duffel on the floor of the foyer as she closed the door, then followed her into the kitchen and took a seat across the table from her. "What's wrong?" he repeated.

"You know there were more dogs than Meat that we rescued from that pit bull fight club, right?" When he nodded, she continued, "Well, while we were at the funeral and repast yesterday, two of the other dogs were stolen from the homes of my coworkers who'd been fostering them. One had been left in a fenced-in backyard with two other dogs that weren't taken—neither of them was a pit bull. Glenn has a doggie door that allows them to go in and out of the house, and he's never had a dog escape from his yard. His neighbor saw a dark SUV pulling out of Glenn's driveway just around noontime but assumed it was one of his friends who often stopped by. She didn't get a good look at the driver or notice if there were any passengers or dogs in the vehicle. The other dog is pregnant and was stolen from Marianne's house—somebody had kicked in the backdoor and taken her. There were no witnesses for that one."

Tuff ran a hand down his face. "Shit. Sounds like the gang is trying to recoup their losses."

"That's what the police think, and we all agree."

A thought crossed Tuff's mind. "I wonder if there's any connection to the guy who vandalized your vehicle."

"That's what I was thinking too. I also thought it might be related to Terry and Megan being murdered."

He'd also thought of that but hadn't wanted to voice it. It was a strong possibility. Those gang members didn't give a crap about anyone who stood in the way of them making money. Taking a life didn't mean a thing to them as long as they got what they wanted. Using the distraction of the funeral to retrieve some of their money-making dogs would've made sense. "Do the homicide detectives know about this?"

She nodded. "Yes, my boss made sure they were notified." She glanced down to where Meat was lying on the floor. "I'll kill anyone who comes for him. I refuse to let those assholes get their hands on him again."

There was no mistaking the venom and determination in her voice. But there was no way Tuff would allow her to be placed in that position. "First thing tomorrow, I'm upgrading your security system. The new cameras and basic system in this unit aren't enough. And I don't want you arguing about it either."

"This time, I'm not going to argue with you. I've learned

my lesson," she said with a little laugh before glancing around. "Um, look, I know it's late, but would you like to have a drink with me? I have some Irish whiskey just waiting to be shared."

Tuff was surprised by her offer, but after a moment's hesitation, he nodded. "Yeah, sure. I could use something to unwind."

He knew he should've turned down the drink, but part of him wasn't ready to leave her yet, especially following the update she'd just given him. After she retrieved the liquor bottle and two lowball glasses from the kitchen cabinets, she gestured toward the living room. "Let's sit in there where it's more comfortable."

Despite knowing the last thing he should do was get more comfortable with Chet, he trailed behind her into the living room and sat on the opposite end of the couch from her. He accepted a half-filled glass and sipped the brown liquid, welcoming the burn in his throat.

"So . . ." Chet started as she turned to face him and crossed her legs Indian style on the couch. "I know you told me you can't talk about some of your assignments, but did everything go okay on this one?"

"Yeah, it did. This wasn't a classified mission, and while I can't name any names, I can say we had to go into Mexico and rescue some guy who'd been kidnapped and held for ransom."

Her eyes widened. "You did? Seriously? Why didn't the cops rescue him?"

"A lot of times, the cops are actually involved down there, so it's best to bring in a private agency like ours. There's no red tape, no law enforcement protocols that have to be followed, nor do we have to worry about a leak giving away our rescue plans. If the bad guys knew we were coming, they'd cut their losses, kill the victim, and be gone long before we got there. Instead, the bad guys thought one of my teammates was bringing the three-million-dollar ransom. They were pretty surprised when things went to shit for them." It'd been a fast op—in and out—which didn't happen often. Now, Tuff was glad it had. He needed to be here if those gang members came looking for Meat, who was snoring from his spot on the floor a few feet away from the couch.

"Three million dollars? Holy crap."

"Yep, and that's one of the cheaper demands I've heard about lately." Not wanting her to ask what had happened to the kidnappers—most were dead, and the few who'd survived wished they were dead—he changed the subject. "So, aside from the dogs going missing, anything else new? Again, I'm sorry I couldn't be there to take you to the funeral yesterday."

She shook her head. "There's nothing to feel sorry about. In fact, I want to thank you for being there for me during the wakes and . . . um . . . and the other night." Her gaze dropped to the narrow area of the couch between them. "I'm the one who should be apologizing."

"Huh? What are you talking about?" He hoped she wasn't about to say what he didn't want her to say . . . that she regretted inviting him into her bed the other night.

"I'm sorry if I embarrassed you or made things awkward between us the other night." She set her glass down on the coffee table. "I just wanted to let you know it meant a lot to me that you were there for me . . . you, know, as a friend."

After setting his barely-touched glass next to hers, he reached out and took her hand in his. "Hey, look at me." He waited until her gaze met his. "There was absolutely nothing embarrassing or awkward about it. I'm glad I was there for you. I just didn't want you to think I was taking advantage of the situation."

A flush crept across her cheeks. "Is that why you didn't . . . um . . . you know . . ." She thought he'd said something along those lines as he'd held her that night before she'd fallen asleep in his arms, but between her post-orgasmic bliss and exhaustion, she wasn't certain.

Chuckling, he rubbed his thumb over her wrist. "Yeah, it is. Trust me, I had a very hard time keeping my pants on, but it had nothing to do with you and everything to do with the circumstances. You're a very beautiful woman, Concetta. Don't ever doubt that."

Butterflies took flight in her stomach at how her full name flowed from his lips in a husky tone. "Thank you." Her chin dipped as she cleared her throat. "I . . . um . . . was wondering, if maybe, you'd . . . uh . . . be interested in maybe, doing—doing it again sometime. I mean, you know, with . . . um . . . both of us getting something out of it."

Tuff's eyebrows shot up as high as they could physically go. That was the last thing he'd expected her to say. She'd shocked the shit out of him, and he couldn't formulate an answer right away. When the silence grew, so did her obvious embarrassment. "I'm sorry, I shouldn't have suggested that. Never mind."

She tried to get to her feet, but he tightened his grip on her hands and pulled until she sat on his lap. "Nope, you're not going anywhere—not after that proposition. I was just stunned for a moment, but now I want to hear more about this idea of yours." So did his damn cock.

Her cheeks were now a deep pink as she fiddled with the hem of her shorts. "Well, I figured, since I'm not dating anyone, and you said, you know, you're not dating anyone, that we could have a sort of friends-with-benefits arrangement. Neither of us wants any commitments, so we could keep it casual. And somewhere down the line, if one of us meets someone, then the two of us will just go back to being friends again. No harm, no foul."

Tuff was an ass. That's the only reason he could give, besides being hard as a rock, for why he said yes.

Chet tilted her head. "Yes... as in..."

He threaded the fingers of one hand through the strands of her hair and pulled her toward him. His lips brushed against hers, sending a shiver through her body and unadulterated lust through his. "Yes, as in I'd be interested in an arrangement like that... with you."

Tuff was going straight to hell—but what a way to go. He should've said no, but if he had, she would've really been embarrassed, and things would have been awkward between them. As much as he wanted this, though, he couldn't help but feel one of them was going to get burned in the end, and it was probably going to be him. But he was done fighting his attraction to her. If this were all he got, a few stolen moments in time when he could pretend she was his, he'd take them and deal with the fallout later.

Without hesitation, Chet opened her mouth. Her tongue peeked out and licked his lips. Tuff smiled and then mimicked her actions. Grasping the hem of her shirt, he dragged it up her torso and over her head, tossing it to the floor. He'd been dreaming of her breasts for the past three days and couldn't wait to get his hands and mouth on them again. Chet rose up on her knees and straddled his hips. Shifting beneath her, Tuff tried to give his aching cock a little more room as she cupped her breasts and offered them to him.

Damn, she was going to be the death of him tonight.

BLACKHAWK SECURITY

CHAPTER FOURTEEN

When Tuff accepted her offering and sucked one rosy-red nipple into his mouth, Chet arched her back. She gasped and held his head to her breasts. This was insane. Absolutely insane. She'd told herself, repeatedly, not to proposition him—she'd only get hurt in the end. But from the moment he'd walked into her house, his bicep brushing against the side of her breast, all thoughts of why she shouldn't go after what she wanted, even in a temporary way, disappeared into thin air. Her body was crackling with electricity and desire just sitting in the same room as him. She wanted him more than any other man she'd ever met, and if she only had a few fleeting moments in her life with him, she'd take them, store them in her memory, and treasure them long after he moved on.

Tuff's teeth bit down lightly on her nipple, and Chet felt it in her core. Her arousal dampened her sleep shorts, reminding her she wasn't wearing any underwear. She hadn't intended to open the door that way, but she'd padded from her bedroom to the kitchen to get a glass of water without putting on a robe moments before she'd heard his truck pull into the driveway. She hadn't wanted to miss him, so she'd hurried to the front door and thrown it open. Now, she was glad she hadn't put on a robe.

Running her hands up his tattooed arms and across his shoulders, she decided he was overdressed. She bunched the material of his shirt in her hands. "Please, Jason, I want to feel your skin. Take this off," she demanded.

She only seemed to call him by his given name when she was aroused and wondered if he even noticed. Releasing her breast, he quickly followed her order, reaching back, grabbing a handful of his shirt, and yanking it over his head. He tossed it toward where he'd thrown her shirt earlier, but it went a little farther than that and ended up draping over half of Meat's big head. The dog was lying on his side, snoring away, and in a true testament to the fact he felt safe in Chet's house, he barely opened his eyes when the shirt landed on him before going back to sleep.

One of Tuff's hands delved into Chet's hair, drawing her closer until his mouth smashed against hers. He teased, tasted, and tantalized her with his tongue and lips. His other arm went around her back, squeezing her until her chest crushed against his. Chet moaned as her nipples hardened even further. The bulge in his pants told her he was just as aroused as she was. She ground her pussy against his cock, soliciting a moan from him.

Putting her hands against his shoulders, she pushed away and climbed off his lap onto her knees in front of him. Heat flared in his eyes as her hands went to the waistband of his shorts. "You don't have to do that, my sweet Concetta." She knew he was referring to a blowjob—he was giving her an out if she was uncomfortable with giving him one—but there was no mistaking the anticipation and need in his voice.

"But I want to." That was no lie—Chet had been dreaming of him fucking her mouth, as well as her pussy, for days. She made quick work of the snap and zipper, eliciting a hiss from him when her fingers brushed against the satiny tip of his hard shaft.

His eyelids fluttered shut as his hips bucked. "God, yes, baby. Touch me, please!"

It was a heady feeling knowing she could make this gorgeous hulk of a man beg. He lifted his hips and helped her push his shorts and boxer briefs down past his knees. His erection bounced against his abdomen, and she took a moment to admire it. Like the man it was attached to, his cock was a thing of beauty. She wrapped her hand around its girth, watching as pre-cum wept from the slit.

Tuff's hand plunged into her hair again, and she lifted her gaze. His nostrils flared, and his jaw was as stiff as his cock. She knew he was holding back, letting her take the lead, not wanting to push her too quickly. Well, he had nothing to worry about—she was completely on board with how fast tonight was going.

Tilting his dick toward her, she leaned down and licked the tip. The hand in her hair tightened, lighting up the nerves in her scalp, but Tuff still didn't take control. She wondered how long he would hold out. This was a man who needed to dominate his sexual encounters, she was sure of it, yet his restraint made her want to push him until he couldn't take it anymore. Her gaze shifted to the side where his other hand clutched the couch's armrest. His knuckles were white.

"Lick me again, baby. Take me into your mouth."

He didn't have to tell her twice. Opening wide, she gave the thick vein on the underside of his cock a swipe of her tongue before closing her lips around the tip and sucking it into her mouth.

"Damn! Oh, shit, don't stop! Mmm, yeah, do that again—just like that." His thin thread of control was slipping, and the hand on her head applied pressure, indicating the pace he wanted her to set. His other hand left the couch and reached out to tease her nipple. A jolt of electricity went straight to her core when he rolled and pulled on the taut peak.

Chet moaned around the hard flesh she was laving and sucking on, then took it to the back of her throat and swallowed. The hand in her hair tightened again as Tuff growled. "Fuck! Let go, woman. If you keep that up, things will be over far too soon."

With a grin, she gave his cock one last swipe before releasing it. "Can't let that happen, now can we?"

Tucking his hands under her shoulders, he helped her to her feet. There was no mistaking the lust in his eyes as he kicked off his sneakers, shorts, and briefs. "Damn straight. I plan on making you come a few times before that happens. Take off those shorts and get up here—stand on the couch. Straddle my hips and put your hands against the wall to steady yourself."

Wide-eyed, she did as she was told, not sure what he planned on doing. Once she was in place, she didn't have to wait long to figure it out. Tuff clutched her hips and pulled them toward him. Leaning his head back against the couch, he settled her pussy over his mouth. *Oh, God!*

His stiff, wet tongue flattened against her labia and licked relentlessly. Thank goodness she had the support of the wall and his strong arms because otherwise, she would've collapsed from the sheer pleasure he was giving her. His big hands kneaded her ass cheeks, alternating between separating them and mashing them together. His tongue whipped her clit in lashes that drove her crazy. It felt so good but wasn't enough to make her climax. Chet bent her knees, grinding herself against his mouth while begging for more, just as Tuff had done moments earlier. "Oh, please! More! Please, more! Ah! Ohhhh! Shit! Please!"

Bringing one hand around, he ran his fingers through her drenched folds, then thrust them inside without warning.

"Shit! Oh, God! Jason!"

His answer was to increase his sensual torture. He sucked on her clit as he finger-fucked her. Chet's legs shook as he drove her higher and higher. She tilted forward, her knees touching the back of the couch by Tuff's ears. She had nothing to hold onto—she could only lean her head and hands against the wall.

"Play with your tits, my sweet bomboncita."

Glancing down, she saw his hungry gaze on her. The lower half of his face was hidden from view as he returned to feasting on her. Leaving the top of her head against the wall as support, she reached down and plucked her nipples, rolling and pulling on them like he'd done earlier. He now had three fingers in her pussy, as his teeth and tongue played with her clit. His other hand snaked between her legs and gathered up some of her cream before returning to the crack of her ass. Chet tensed. She'd never had a man touch her there before.

"Relax, baby. It's not going to hurt. I'm just going to rim this pretty hole and stimulate you a bit. I won't try to enter you. We'll save that for another time. Just relax and feel."

"The feel part I can dooooo," she moaned as he put just a little pressure on her asshole and sucked on her clit simultaneously. His fingers between her legs never stopped fucking her. "Oh, *Dios mio*! But I'm ssssstrung too tight to r-relax. Oh! Please, Jason!"

"Please, what, baby? Tell me what you want."

Damn, he was the chattiest guy during sex she'd ever been with. Most of the men she'd dated, including her ex-husband, had just wanted to get on with it. Then again, none of them had ever had her stand over them on the couch while they tortured her with their fingers, mouths, tongues, and teeth.

"Concetta, tell me. Do you want me to slow down?"

"Oh, God, don't you dare!" She was almost there—just a little more.

"Then tell me what you want, baby. Say it."

"Oh, damn it!" she cried out on a sob. "Please, let me come!"

Again, his response was non-verbal. He stroked inside her, faster, harder. The finger at her back hole teased just enough to get her attention. But what sent her over was when Tuff sucked her clit between his teeth and lightly bit down. "Ahhhhhhh! Oh, my God! Oh, my God! Oh, shit!"

Her whole body shook, and the only reason she didn't fall was that Tuff's hand left her ass and wrapped around her, clutching her opposite hip and holding her in place. His mouth and fingers drew out her orgasm until she finally sagged against the wall.

Somehow, Tuff lowered her to the couch and crawled on Over her. His erection nestled against her pussy, but he didn't thrust inside her. Instead, he turned his attention to her nipples, laving one and then the other. Chet hadn't thought it was possible, but she began climbing the cliff of ecstasy again. Never in her life had she had multiple orgasms this close together, but then again, never in her life had she been with a man like Tuff. He was so attentive to her needs and desires, putting his own on hold. He'd said he wanted to give her several orgasms before experiencing his own, and she'd thought it was just something he'd spouted out during foreplay. But now she knew he'd not only been serious but confident he could follow through with his statement.

As he leaned on his forearms above her, his hips pumped, rubbing his cock over her sensitive clit. The next orgasm hit her without warning, and she screamed his name as wave after wave crashed over her. In a fog, she barely registered Tuff retrieving a condom from his discarded shorts and rolling it onto his stiff shaft. Leaning down, he brushed his lips across hers. "Last chance to back out, Concetta. I want you so fucking bad right now, but if it's not what you want, tell me now, and I'll go take care of things in the shower."

"Don't you fucking dare, Tuff." She lifted her pelvis to his. "I want you too. Now!"

"Demanding little thing, aren't you?"

"Damn straight," she said with a grin, repeating his words from earlier.

He lined the tip of his cock with her slit, then eased inside. Chet's passage welcomed him as she wrapped her legs around his hips. Tuff's eyes slammed shut, and his body tensed with restraint. "Shit! You're so fucking tight—like a glove. So hot and wet."

"Don't hold back." Biting her lip, she dug her heels into his ass, urging him on.

"I don't want to hurt you, baby."

Chet shook her head back and forth on the couch cushion. "You're not. You're driving me crazy!"

One or two more thrusts and he was balls deep inside her. He held himself there. "One sec, honey, otherwise I won't last."

She gave him more than "one sec," but no more than five before she clenched around him in her core. "Please! I need you to move."

Retreating, he plunged back in, setting a slow pace that soon started a third orgasm building inside her. *Holy shit!* This one wasn't the fast rush of the one before it, but a slow, lazy trip, higher and higher to where she would fly once again.

Putting most of his weight on one arm, he used the fingers of the opposite hand to pinch her nipple. The pleasure/pain shot through her, sending her tumbling into an abyss. His pubic bone bounced off her clit, prolonging her climax. "That's it, baby. Take me with you."

With one final thrust, Tuff came with a growling roar. Moments later, he collapsed on top of her. She welcomed the solid weight of him, despite the fact they were both gasping for oxygen.

Tuff gently kissed her temple, and Chet tried to ignore how the simple gesture expanded her heart.

Damn it! Stop falling for him!

Unfortunately, that was easier said than done.

CHAPTER FIFTEEN

Three weeks later...

Chet opened her work locker and found the bottle of Tylenol she kept there just in case she got a headache. And, boy, did she have one now, and the day had barely started. Day five of training the new guy, and she was going nuts. Twenty-four-year-old Leo Price was a nice enough kid, but he *never* shut up! *Never!*

There had been times during the past week when Chet had just wanted to yell, "Shut the fuck up for five fucking minutes!" It was almost like having a six-year-old in the vehicle with her, asking why questions, one after the other. Then when he wasn't asking questions, he was droning on and on about one hobby or another, a life experience, something he'd read, or any other thing that'd popped into his mind. Thank God all next week, he'd be over at the police academy, going through the firearms training with the new TPD recruits. She'd get a five-day reprieve—nine with the two weekends thrown in there—to try and recover her sanity.

At least she had something to look forward to. Tuff was getting home tomorrow, sometime around noon, from the out-of-town assignment he was on. He'd texted her last night to see if she wanted to go to a new movie they both had been looking forward to seeing. The friends-with-benefits arrangement they'd started had strengthened the "friendship" part of their relationship. They'd started to hang out together more often. Twice they'd taken Meat to visit a dog-friendly section of the beach on the Gulf, another time, they'd gone out for pizza and a beer, while a few nights, they'd shared cooking and cleaning duties at her place. Most of those times, they'd ended up in bed together, and holy hell, did that man know how to please a woman, or what? With Tuff, multiple orgasms had become a regular occurrence for Chet.

While the sex was amazing, and she loved hanging out with him, Chet knew she would have to end it soon. Her heart was way too involved now—she hadn't been able to help it. She was falling in love with a man who'd made it clear he didn't feel the same. Whenever they'd had sex, he'd stayed for a little bit afterward, cuddling and talking, but after she'd fallen asleep in his arms, he'd extricated himself and gone back to his own place. Each time, Chet woke up alone, feeling disappointed, but she wasn't ready to let go of him and return to being just friends yet. A few more days, maybe a few more weeks, then she'd have to extricate herself from their sex life—it was the only way to stop her heart from being ripped to shreds when he decided it was time to move on. Hopefully, she hadn't passed that point already—*dream on, Chet.*

Popping two caplets into her mouth, Chet washed them down with the iced coffee she'd picked up on her way to work. After closing her locker, she headed for the door. She wanted to make sure Meat was comfortable in Des's office before her shift started—he was one of the few men the dog appeared comfortable with.

Poor Meat. He'd had his teeth cleaned and an abscess on his gums removed the other day and was still taking pain meds. When Chet had picked him up from the vet, he'd still been loopy from the anesthesia and had been so damn cute, walking like a drunken sailor. She'd sent Tuff a video of him in the backyard through Messenger, and he'd responded:

TUFF

"Bwahahahaha. Too cute. Give the poor guy an ear scratch from me."

Texting back and forth with Tuff was another thing Chet would have to curb. It was becoming too natural to want to tell him everything that happened throughout her day—whether it was good or bad. She had plenty of friends, but for some reason, Tuff was the first person she texted about anything lately. He called and texted her often as well, especially if he was out of town. She knew he was worried about her, but since Terry and Megan's funeral, nothing had happened to the other fight club dogs still being fostered through several rescue groups. It probably helped that the suspected leader of the gang, Jose Martinez, was behind bars again. He'd been released on bail for the list of charges that had stemmed from the raid on his home, but two weeks ago, he'd been arrested again on drug charges. Chet hoped the bastard would stay in jail until his trial.

Unfortunately, the police hadn't been able to connect Martinez to the dognappings or the murders of Terry and Megan. As it stood now, they believed the latter was either a road rage thing or a case of mistaken identity. As for the dognappings, they were pretty sure Martinez was involved and had also been responsible for the vandalism of Chet's

SUV, but again, without proof, they couldn't charge him with any of that.

As Leo exited the men's locker room and spotted her striding down the hallway, Chet sighed inwardly. Her trainee grinned. "Morning, Chet, whatta we doin' today?"

"I'll meet you at the truck in a few minutes—you can start the equipment checklist. We've got a bunch of follow-up calls to deal with."

A flash of disappointment appeared on the younger man's freckled face before disappearing again. Chet had quickly learned Leo preferred active rescue or intervention calls rather than ones just requiring paperwork and interviews. *Suck it up, buttercup. Grunt work is part of every freaking job, even this one.*

After checking on Meat and being reassured Des would take good care of him again today, Chet helped Leo finish making sure their truck had all the equipment they might need during the day. Even though the ACOs were supposed to replenish supplies before the end of their shift, they still had a checklist that needed to be completed each morning.

Climbing into the driver's seat, Chet started the vehicle just as the dashboard police radio squelched. "Headquarters to ACO-7."

Before she could reach for the transmitter, Leo enthusiastically snatched it from its perch and responded, "ACO-7."

"ACO-7, need you to respond to one-five-nine-eight Kaufman Drive and assist officers there. They're out with an elderly party who fell, but her German Shepard isn't letting them in the house to help her."

"Not again," Chet groaned as she put the truck in gear and pulled out of the parking spot. "Tell them our ETA is five minutes."

"ACO-7 to headquarters, we copy that. ETA is five minutes."

"Ten-four," the dispatcher acknowledged.

Twenty minutes later, the elderly woman was en route to the ER with a broken arm and a deep laceration on her forehead that would require stitches, while her German Shepard, George, was in one of the ACO truck's kennels. The dog had calmed down once he'd spotted a familiar face and allowed Chet to open the front door and attach a leash to his collar. She'd then taken him outside so EMS could tend to his mistress. Mrs. Kensington was a sweet lady, but this was the eighth or ninth call for assistance in the past three months at the address. Unfortunately, she'd been resisting her family's request that she move into an assisted living facility. She wouldn't be allowed to bring George due to his size—smaller dogs and cats were allowed. As she'd done in the past, Chet drove the dog to a local Camp Bow Wow. Mrs. Kensington's son, who had a thirty-minute drive to the ER from work, would pick the dog up later.

As soon as they radioed the dispatcher that they were back in service, Chet and Leo were dispatched to a loose dog complaint. Chet got the impression it would be one of those days when they worked their tails off—pun intended. At least it would keep her mind off Tuff and the inevitable countdown toward the end of their FWB relationship.

BLACKHAWK SECURITY

CHAPTER SIXTEEN

Striding down the hallway on the tenth floor of a downtown Miami office building, where an asset was in a secure conference room one floor above, Tuff checked each door knob, assuring himself they were all still locked. It was after 2:00 p.m. on a Saturday, and the seventh through eleventh floors were empty except for security—the computer company's own staff and the men from Blackhawk—and the eight people in the closed-door meeting. The six members of Tuff's team didn't know what new software or hardware was being discussed nor the dollar amounts negotiated—it was probably well over one million—but it really didn't matter to them. All that *did* matter was making sure their Chinese client was returned to his private jet at the end of the meeting without being harmed. Many times, Tuff wondered if anyone really had some of their assets in their crosshairs for one reason or another, but the team still had to be ready for anything.

Entering a stairwell, he took the steps two at a time to the next floor. Before opening the door, he activated the microphone on his comms unit. "Dusty. Chaos. I'm at the stairwell door."

"Copy that, Tuff," Kyle "Chaos" Grant responded. "You're clear."

Now that his teammates knew one of their own was making an appearance, Tuff wouldn't be looking at any drawn weapons when he entered the hallway. Pulling the door open, he strode through, looked left, then right, assessing everything in mere seconds. Dustin "Dusty" Gibson and one of the on-site armed guards were stationed at the elevator, which had been disabled from the main security office on the second floor. Marty "Sherlock" Holmes was in charge of the detail, with Tuff being second-in-command, and was down there, monitoring the surveillance feeds with the head of security.

At the other end of the hallway, a guard stood with Grant at the door to the conference room. Tuff's usual partner, Blane "Boots" Nelson, and Vinnie "Reaper" Burke were in the driver's seats of two SUVs, sitting in a no-parking zone on the north side of the building. Since the company's multi-level parking lot was across the street from the main entrance, the side exit was as close as they could get to the building without driving up on the sidewalk. The team had used Blackhawk's contacts with MPD to ensure they wouldn't be hassled by anyone on patrol or from the Miami Parking Authority. Hopefully, they'd be leaving soon and taking their asset back to the airport.

As soon as their client was airborne on a long flight back to China, the BHS team would head over to the Miami International Airport Hotel, where they had rooms waiting for them. After changing out of their work clothes and gear, they'd head out for a few hours of late afternoon fishing before hitting a bar in South Beach for some beers and dinner. In the morning, they'd meet an international flight from Munich that was transporting the very expensive, frozen sperm of four highly sought-after German Shepard sires, which would be used to impregnate several bitches in BHS's breeding program. Kat Michaelson had clients already interested in the trained pups with strong lineage resulting from the pairings.

Striding down the hallway toward Grant, Tuff asked, "Think they're almost done? We were supposed to be out of here an hour ago."

"Yeah, one of them came out to use the restroom about ten minutes ago and said they were wrapping things up."

Just as Grant finished saying that, the door next to him swung open, and an executive in his mid-forties stuck his head out. "We're done, gentlemen. You're all set to escort Mr. Chin back to the airport."

Inside the boardroom, the thirty-seven-year-old man Tuff's team was protecting closed the latches of his briefcase before picking it up and walking toward the door. Tuff held up his hand. "Mr. Chin, please give us just a moment to confirm we're all clear downstairs, and then we'll be on our way."

"Of course," he replied in mildly-accented English. While it was clear he was wealthy and well-educated, his personality belied his outward appearance. Unlike the men he'd met with, who were wearing chinos and button-down Oxfords, Chin was dressed in a custom-fit, gray, three-piece suit. Tuff was positive the man's shiny shoes cost at least $1500, while the Rolex on his wrist went for at least three times that amount. Yet, he'd been very polite to his security team and had even conversed and joked with them on the ride from the airport—something many assets couldn't be bothered with. "I apologize for the meeting running so late."

"No problem, sir, it goes with the territory." Tuff activated his microphone again. "Bones, Sherlock, we're ready to move out. Are we clear?"

Both men replied, "Affirmative."

Within two minutes, Gibson was in one elevator with two of the in-house guards, en route to the lobby, with Tuff, Grant, and their asset following in a second one. Gibson would meet up with Holmes and make sure the lobby and the side exit to where the vehicles were waiting were clear before they'd let their client out of the elevator.

As the car descended, Chin used the fingers of one hand to respond to a text on his smartphone. He glanced at Tuff. "Mr. Tanner, since I won't be using the main terminal at the airport, may I impose upon you to stop along the way at any little shop that carries toys? My daughter would like me to bring her home a present."

He smiled. "I don't think that will be a problem. I highly doubt anyone would be waiting in one on the off chance your daughter wanted you to bring her something. I'll let the team know once we're in the vehicles, and then I'll locate a store nearby."

"Thank you."

While he had no children, Tuff couldn't help but think about bringing home a new toy for Meat. Of course, it would have to be from a pet store and something the pit bull wouldn't rip apart in the first few minutes. Not only was Tuff missing Chet, but he was missing the big lug too. Meat was much more comfortable around him now, along with a few of the men Chet worked with, but he was still a little aggressive when strange men or someone he didn't know well approached. Chet was working on that, and Kat Michaelson had invited her to bring Meat to the Trident compound one day, where they could work on socializing the dog some more while in a controlled setting.

At least Tuff didn't have to worry about Chet and Meat's

safety with the head of the dog fighting ring behind bars again. Tuff was certain he'd been to blame for the dognappings and the damage to Chet's vehicle that night, but he agreed with Isaac Webb about the murders of Chet's friends. While they wouldn't put it past Martinez to use violence to get what he wanted, since Terry hadn't been fostering one of the rescued pit bulls, it didn't make sense for the bastard to go after him. That, and the fact that no one else had been injured when the two dogs had been taken from their foster homes.

The elevator dinged, announcing their arrival on the first floor. When the door opened, Chin tucked his phone back into the inside pocket of his suit jacket, then followed Tuff and Grant out into the lobby, where they turned left. Tuff let the asset pass and got behind him while Grant led the way. Holmes was waiting at the side door. Gibson was already outside, waiting by the first SUV that Chin, Tuff, and Grant would climb into. Holmes and Gibson would ride with Burke and follow the others.

Due to several round concrete barriers spaced a few feet apart along the curb, and an extra-wide sidewalk, there was about fifteen feet between the exit and the first SUV with its closest rear door wide open. Unfortunately, at that time of the evening, people were bustling up and down the side street of the business district. Some were heading to the railway station two blocks over, while others were walking home from work or heading to dinner or a night out on the town. Taxis, trucks, and cars drove down the one-way street, and several bicyclists cruised by. Exiting the building, Tuff, Grant, and Holmes surrounded Chin, escorting him to the waiting SUV.

The roar of a small engine caught Tuff's attention. Turning his head in the direction it was coming from, he saw something very out of place. A motorcycle was speeding down the sidewalk, instead of in the street, headed straight toward them. From that point, everything seemed to go in slow motion. Gibson yelled, "Gun!" at the same time, Tuff saw the helmeted driver of the bike aim a black handgun at Chin. As Holmes, Gibson, and Tuff drew their weapons, Grant got between the threat and the asset, practically shoving Chin into the backseat as the assailant fired his weapon three times.

There were far too many innocent pedestrians screaming and confused about which direction they should run in for the team to return fire. Tuff barely dove out of the way in time as the heavy motorcycle approached him. Holmes managed to pull a young woman out of harm's way as the bike flew past them. Burke exited the rear SUV with his gun drawn and his cell to his ear, yelling at a 9-1-1 dispatcher that shots had been fired and they had a man down. Rolling to his feet, Tuff stomach sank as he saw Grant on the ground, blood squirting into the air from his neck. Tuff lunged forward to render aid, slapping his hand over the arterial wound as Holmes started barking out orders. "Gibson! Burke! Get the asset out of here!"

The men had been jumping into the back of the first vehicle, sandwiching an uninjured Chin between them as soon as their team leader had said their names. Every man knew his role if the shit hit the fan—the asset was to be protected at all costs. Nelson floored the accelerator before the doors were even shut, taking Chin to a predetermined safehouse until arrangements could be made to get him out of the country safely. Holmes and Tuff would take care of their injured teammate.

Several armed guards from the computer company came running to help. One of them fell to his knees next to Tuff with a first-aid duffel. He immediately began pulling out sterile gauze pads, ripping open the packages, and handing them to Tuff, who'd been using his bare hands to try and stem the flow of blood. The other two bullets had hit Grant in the back and been stopped by the bullet-proof vest he'd been wearing under a lightweight jacket. All the team members had been wearing them for this very reason—they never knew when a job would go FUBAR like this one just had.

Holmes and the five other guards stood watch over them, watching for the assailant in case he returned to do more damage They also prevented any lookie-loos from getting gruesome videos or photos of the injured operative.

Lying on his stomach, Grant was conscious and gasping for air but wasn't moving otherwise. It finally clicked in Tuff's head that his teammate could be paralyzed from the neck down. The bullet must have sliced through his spine before nicking his carotid artery. Grant had lost far too much blood, and the approaching sirens couldn't get there fast enough for Tuff, who was doing all he could to save his friend and teammate. He didn't want to risk further damage by rolling Grant onto his back without the proper equipment the medics would be bringing.

"T-Tuff?"

He barely heard Grant's voice over the commotion around them and leaned down to hear him better. "Yeah, Chaos, I'm here. Help's on the way. We'll get you out of here as soon as we can."

"T-tell Bec . . . Becca . . . I . . ." He coughed up blood, and it spattered on the concrete. Several police cars and an ambulance came screaming onto the scene, and Tuff had to lower his head even more to hear Grant. "Tell her . . . I . . . love her . . . s-so sor . . . sorry."

The retired Marine was dying, and there wasn't anything anyone could do to stop it. Grant knew it. Tuff knew it. So did everyone with military or law enforcement experience around them. Tuff had been in this position too many times to count, mostly in combat on the other side of the world. He knew better than to give Grant false platitudes that everything would be all right, that he'd pull through. They wouldn't be any comfort to the dying man. Tuff told him what he needed to hear—that his fiancée would know his last thoughts were of her. "I'll tell her, Kyle. I'll make sure she knows how much you love her. Your folks and brothers too. I'll tell them all."

His eyes filled with tears as Grant released his final breath seconds before the medics pushed through the crowd to work on him. Even though there was nothing they could do for the man, Tuff moved out of their way. They had to at least try to save him, but the looks on their faces said they didn't have much hope.

Getting to his feet, Tuff stared at his hands, covered in his friend's blood. Holmes stepped over to him with his cell phone in hand and an anguished look on his face. "The asset's secure. Chase and Irv are on their way. We have to give our statements to the cops—they'll keep Kyle's name out of the press." As black-ops agents with military and government clearance, they often had their names withheld from reports and press releases for classified reasons. While this had been a private security detail, Chase would do whatever he could to make sure Kyle's name was kept quiet so his fiancée and family didn't have to deal with the onslaught of reporters knocking on their doors. It wouldn't be the first time they gave the press a fake name and identity, and it probably wouldn't be the last.

Unable to find his voice just then, Tuff nodded as he watched the medics' futile efforts as they placed Grant on a backboard and then a gurney before continuing CPR on the way to the back of the ambulance. Already, in his mind, he was trying to figure out what he would say to the man's fiancée and parents—Chase and Irv would go with him to do the notification, but Tuff would tell them Grant's dying words. He was dreading the moment when they would learn their loved one was never coming home.

Turning, he strode back into the building, needing a few minutes to gather himself before his rage and sorrow overtook him. An image of Chet flashed through his mind. He had to break things off with her. Tuff could never let her go through what Becca Reyes and the Grant family would be going through by the end of the day. He cared too much for her to engage her in a relationship where she might, very well, get the notification he wasn't coming home someday.

Unable to stop himself, Tuff punched the nearest wall.

CHAPTER SEVENTEEN

"What's next?" Chase asked, glancing at a piece of paper in front of him with the meeting's agenda on it.

Sitting on the other side of the BHS owner's desk, Ian Sawyer consulted his own list of topics he'd wanted to cover with his business associate. "I need you to head to D.C. with me next month to finalize everything with the NSA. Once everyone signs on the dotted line, we can patch you into our interface. Cookie will have to monitor all requests and the resulting intel—the brass wouldn't budge on that. You and I can figure out what it all works out to in trade later."

Trident Security had hit the jackpot last year when they'd been able to lure one of the top computer geeks at the National Security Agency into the private sector. With TS's high-clearance levels and black-ops government contracts, one of the perks of the deal had been Nathan Cook could maintain his access to the NSA's mainframe computers. Since Chase had similar contracts with Uncle Sam, he'd approached Sawyer and the bigwigs in Washington about gaining access to information that could be vital for missions.

After months of negotiations and everyone at BHS going under the proverbial microscope, they'd finally gotten the thumbs up. Instead of money constantly going back and forth between BHS and TS, as the latter company grew over the past few years, the owners usually kept track of who owed what, and it was usually paid back in personnel, equipment, intel, or anything else they could come up with.

"Okay—I'll have Shannon get Colleen on the phone and let them set up the meetings and travel details." He made a few notes on the paper to have his secretary contact Ian's. "Anything else?"

Ian tossed his leather-covered day planner onto the empty chair next to him. "Last thing I've got is my dipshits want to challenge your dipshits to a softball game sometime in the next month or two. It was Egghead's idea, and from there, it spread like a bad breakout of VD. I did nix his suggestion for what the losers would have to do, though, because I wasn't taking any chances—don't ask."

Chase chuckled. "I won't, but—"

A knock at his door, followed by it swinging open, cut off what he'd been about to say. Irv strode in, being the only person in the office who wouldn't have waited for permission to enter. The six-foot-five retired Green Beret was frowning, but there was no urgency in his demeanor. He stopped behind the empty guest chair and rested his hands on the back of it. "Sorry for the interruption, but Tuff just banged out again. Told me to keep him off the schedule until further notice. When I tried to talk to him, he told me to fuck off—sounded a tad drunk, so I'll let it slide until he's sober enough to feel the pain I plan to inflict upon his ass."

"Fuck," Chase murmured, running a hand down his face.

Raising an eyebrow, Ian asked, "Hasn't been back to work since?"

He let out a heavy sigh. "Nope."

It'd been over two weeks since Kyle Grant's funeral, and as expected, BHS's operatives and support staff were still mourning, but Tuff had taken it the hardest. Chase understood how his employee felt. He'd had several men die in his arms over the years, both in and out of the military—unfortunately, it came with the territory. He also knew that if he allowed Tuff to wallow in his sorrow for too long, he might never get over his misplaced guilt and return to the job he loved and needed.

Chase was a tough-as-nails boss but cared about every one of his employees—from the operatives down to the cleaning staff that came in at night under the watchful eyes of security guards—to give them some leeway with their personal lives. He also knew when to tighten the reins. He'd already lost one good operative this month and wasn't about to lose another to unwarranted guilt. He'd read the reports, backward and forward, and debriefed the entire team over several days. Irv and the intel staff had gotten the surveillance videos from every available camera within a two-block radius of the shooting. The BHS team had done nothing wrong. They'd gotten the asset out of there alive. Chase wouldn't have done a damn thing differently if he'd been the team leader on that detail. It'd been just lousy luck that only five out of the six operatives had made it home. It was also a fluke that his and Sawyer's teams had already tracked down the Russian-born assassin, who was wanted by most international government agencies, and had handed him over to Deimos, a blacker-than-black-ops US agency. They would dispose of the body once they'd tortured some intel from the fucking bastard. The only reason the BHS operatives hadn't done it themselves was because Deimos was sanctioned—in other words, it wouldn't be murder.

Tossing the pen he'd been holding onto his desk, Chase eyed Ian. "You in the mood to go kick some sense into his ass with me?"

A wide grin spread across the retired SEAL's face as he stood and clapped his hands once before rubbing them together. "I thought you'd never ask."

Picking up her handbag, phone, and keys, Chet glanced around, ensuring she had everything. With her mother arriving tomorrow, she'd taken the day off, along with the rest of the week. She was so excited to see her mom, but part of her still felt frustrated about Tuff. It looked like their friends-with-benefits arrangement was over earlier than she'd reckoned it would be and not because she'd ended it. Tuff had. Well, at least she assumed he had.

She hadn't seen him much during the past three weeks, even though his truck was almost always in the driveway. The night they were supposed to go to the movies, one of his teammates had been killed earlier in the day. He'd come home a wreck and shut her out moments after giving her the news when she'd met him on the front porch. Chet didn't know exactly what'd happened—she'd searched the internet with what little she knew but couldn't find any incidents she could connect to Tuff or Blackhawk Security. Whatever had happened, it'd been kept very quiet.

Ever since then, Tuff had ignored most of her texts and phone calls and rarely answered if she knocked on his door to check on him. The few times he had, she almost hadn't recognized him. He hadn't shaved, and his hair had grown out a little. His clothes had been unkempt, his eyes red, and she'd suspected he'd been drinking—a lot. At first, she'd tried to comfort him. When that hadn't worked, she'd decided to give him a little space. Unfortunately, that space now felt like a mile-wide chasm. She knew a few of his friends had stopped by, but apparently, they'd gotten similar treatment. Tuff wanted to be alone with his alcohol and the takeout deliveries that arrived occasionally. He didn't even sit out on his back porch anymore.

She missed him—more than she'd expected. Somewhere along the line, despite her resistance, she'd fallen in love with the man, and now he wanted nothing to do with her.

Sighing, she grabbed Meat's leash and attached it to his collar. "Well, boy, if you have any suggestions on how to get through to Mister Thick Skull next door, let me know. In the meantime, whatta you say we hit the dog spa and then the grocery store? I'll lock the doors, leave the AC cranking for you, and just run in for milk, eggs, and chicken. If anyone is stupid enough to try and steal my truck, then they deserve whatever you do to them."

"Woof!" She'd been surprised when Meat had seemed to enjoy his recent bath at a local dog spa. Instead of trying to wrestle him into her tub, she'd taken him to the spa, where they had ramps for the dogs to walk up into oversized sinks. Chet didn't have to bend over to bathe him, and the goofball had groaned in ecstasy as she'd massaged the shampoo into his coat and then rinsed it off with warm water. He'd then spent the ride home rolling around on an old blanket she'd laid out for him in the back of her SUV.

Holding the leash tightly in one hand, she opened the door with the other. To her surprise, Meat lunged forward, barking and growling at two strange men standing in front of Tuff's door, and she was thankful she had a good grip on the nylon strap in her hand as she tried to calm the dog down. "Ruhig."

Both men were in their early to mid-forties, wearing tan cargo pants and black T-shirts, each with a different logo over the left side of their chests. One took two wary steps backward while eyeing the big dog. Like Tuff had been the day he'd met Meat, the man looked like he could react instantly, vaulting over the banister. His salt-and-pepper crewcut, toned physique, sharp green eyes, and commanding presence screamed military. While the man didn't scare her for some reason, Chet knew he probably had his enemies shaking in their boots.

The other man, however, who'd barely moved a muscle, was intimidating without saying a word. With jet-black hair, piercing blue eyes, a ridiculously handsome face, and lean, rock-hard muscles from head to toe, he undoubtedly had women falling to their knees in front of him. Instead of altering his stance, he held his position and stared at Meat. He wasn't challenging the dog but establishing his dominance. Shocked, Chet watched as Meat backed up, his head and now-wagging tail dropping in submission. His barks and growls turned into whines and woofs as he shifted back and forth on his paws.

Moving slowly, the man opened one of the many pockets on his tan pants and removed a small, clear bag holding what looked like bits of beef jerky. He pulled out a piece. "*Sitz.*"

To Chet's amazement, Meat followed the German command and sat beside her. After making sure the dog was staying in his ordered position, the man tossed the treat so Meat could easily snatch it out of the air without standing again. Two bites and it was gone. Meat leaned forward, sniffing, probably wishing another piece was coming.

Chet stared at the man. "I hope that was organic and not some junk with preservatives in it."

His blue eyes sparkled as the corners of his mouth ticked upward. His voice was deep and tinged with amusement when he said, "Since the woman who trains my dogs hands me an invoice every month for some very expensive treats that cost more than the whole side of beef, I'm going to say it's organic. And yes, I'm certain she's not switching it out for junk food. Kat's very trustworthy."

"Kat? Kat Michaelson?"

"Mm-hmm. Her husband works for me. Even though she trains my dogs, she won't let me call her an employee. She prefers 'contract agent.' Since the dogs love her, and she makes me money, I let her have her way in that matter." He extended his hand. "Ian Sawyer."

She shook the offered hand, feeling the strength he was keeping in check for her. "Chet Suarez."

When she glanced at the other man, he stepped forward and also extended his hand. "Chase Dixon. Nice to meet you."

"Um, nice to meet you too. You're Tuff's boss, right?"

"And you must be the woman who he upgraded the security around here for." He grinned as his gaze did a quick down-and-up scan of her body before returning to her face. "Now I can see why. He's got good taste."

Her eyes widened slightly, and a blush stole across her face when she realized he was complimenting her. She didn't get the impression he was flirting with her and trying to make a move on an employee's woman, more like just stating the fact he found her attractive and there was nothing more to it. But then again, she wasn't Tuff's woman. She never had been and didn't know how to classify herself now that their friendship seemed to have waned as well.

"He hasn't exactly been showing his face lately. I hope you're here to help him. He's been depressed, I assume, about your other agent and doesn't want to talk about it. I'm sorry for your loss."

Dixon's gaze softened. "Thank you, and don't worry, we'll take care of Tuff. It comes with the territory in our business, unfortunately." He tilted his head and eyed Meat. "Is everything else all right around here? Tuff filled me in on what was going on with this big guy. You're an ACO, right?"

She glanced down at the dog, whose tongue was lolling out as he gazed adoringly at Sawyer. Chet shook her head in awe and amusement. This was the first man who'd ever gotten this kind of response from Meat since she'd rescued him. Sawyer just exuded dominance, and for some reason, the dog didn't feel threatened by it.

"Yes, I am. Things seemed to have quieted down. The other dogs that were recovered from the fight club have been fostered out of state for their protection and for those who'd been taking care of them. There haven't been any other incidents. I tried to send Meat somewhere safe out of state two weeks ago, but the woman fostering him said he was very depressed and wouldn't eat. After a few days, I had to get him, and now he's back to normal. I hadn't planned on being his forever mom, but apparently, he has a different opinion."

She'd missed the dog something awful and hated sending him away, but she'd tried to do the right thing to keep him safe. Meat, however, seemed to think his safe place was with Chet.

Pulling a small card out of his wallet, Dixon handed it to her. "If Tuff's not around and you need anything, call my office and tell them who you are. I'll make sure you get any help you need." He held his hand out for Meat to sniff, and after a moment, the dog licked it. "My sister fosters pit bulls up in Pennsylvania, and we were raised with a few Staffordshire terriers, so I've got a soft spot for them."

"Thank you." She tucked the card in her purse, then jutted her chin toward Tuff's door. "Good luck with him. Tell him ... tell him I'm here if he wants to talk." She was embarrassed that her voice broke on the last few words. Swallowing hard, she looked down at Meat. "You ready to go run our errands, boy?"

"*Woof!*"

The two men grinned and stepped to the side so she could descend the stairs with the dog, who gave Sawyer a final sniff before following her. When she reached her SUV, she glanced back and found both men watching her. Oddly, they didn't knock on Tuff's door as she pulled out of the driveway and then drove away. She really hoped they could get through to him. Even though he didn't want a romantic relationship with her, she'd be willing to have a platonic friendship with him.

Yeah, keep telling yourself that, Chet, and maybe someday you'll believe it.

BLACKHAWK SECURITY

CHAPTER EIGHTEEN

Tuff jolted awake, confused and panicked. That's what happens when you're hit in the face with a bucketful of ice water. In an automatic reflex, he reached for his weapon on the nightstand next to his bed but came up empty-handed. His bloodshot eyes finally focused, and relief and then anger coursed through him when he saw his boss and Sawyer grinning down at him. Chase had Tuff's gun in his hand and placed it back where he'd picked it up from while the other bastard was holding the now-empty bucket he'd pulled out of the kitchen pantry. "Get your ass up, twatsicle!"

Rolling to the other side of the king-sized bed where it was a lot dryer—well, at least, less wet—Tuff closed his eyes against the waves of nausea that came over him. His hair, face, and torso were drenched, and he removed his T-shirt, tossing the soaked garment to the floor without caring about the carpet. He laid back down and covered his eyes with his forearm. His head pounded, and his tongue felt thick and dry. "Get the fuck out of my house."

"Not happening," Chase responded in a matter-of-fact

tone. "I've given you over two weeks to get your head squared away, but since you're obviously having a hard time doing that, consider this an intervention. Get up."

Tuff growled and refused to follow the barked order. He wasn't in the military anymore and couldn't get thrown in the stockade for failing to obey a superior's command—at the most, he'd get fired or his ass kicked. Neither was a great option, but both were definitely better than Leavenworth. Maybe if he ignored them, they'd go away.

"Get up, Tuff," his boss repeated. "We're heading over to the Trident compound for some training."

"Fuck that. I told Irv I'm taking a leave of absence. Now, get—"

His words were cut off when he was hit in the face with another bucketful of water, this time sans ice. Sawyer must have used it all from Tuff's freezer the first time.

"God fucking damn it!" He bolted from the bed and almost face-planted as the room spun. Leaning against his dresser, he bent over with his hands on his knees, taking deep breaths and trying to control his nausea as water dripped from his nose, chin, and hair. "Are you fucking kidding me?"

"Yeah, twatsicle, we're fucking kidding you. This was all a silly, high-school prank. You can go back to bed now. Nighty-night."

Sarcasm was Ian Sawyer's middle name, and right then, Tuff hated the man. Standing upright, he glared at the retired SEAL. "You're an asshole, you know that?"

"Nope, Egghead's the asshole. How many times do I have to remind you idiots?" He tossed the empty bucket on the soaked bed. "Unless you want it to fucking reek in here, I'd put those sheets and stuff in the dryer. Then get dressed. Your ass is ours for the rest of the day."

"And if I refuse?"

Chase shrugged. "Ian was telling me Mistress China has a new, hot-pink whip she's been using. We'll just tie you to one of those cross things . . ." He glanced at Sawyer. "Who are they named after again?"

"St. Andrew." Standing there, with his arms crossed over his chest, Sawyer blocked Tuff's only escape route unless he chose to dive through a window. The look in the man's eyes was a combination of anger and understanding. Most of the anger was probably aimed at the situation and not Tuff. Kyle had worked a few contracts with Trident Security, just like Tuff and other BHS operatives had. All the members of both Trident Security teams and their spouses or significant others had attended the wakes and the funeral unless they'd been out of town on missions. A few had gotten back in time for the services, but others were deep undercover and may not even be aware of Kyle's death yet.

"A kinky saint?"

"He was a martyr."

"Whatever," Chase said while shaking his head before returning his attention to Tuff. "Anyway, we'll just tie you to one of those babies and let the sadistic Domme beat your ass."

Shit. Pretty much every contract operative who'd done work for Trident knew the Sawyer brothers, and many of their employees were into BDSM. In fact, there was an elite club, The Covenant, in one of four warehouses at the compound. Unless someone were told it was there, they'd never know it. Tuff had been inside it a few times when it'd been closed, and the rich decor was in direct contrast to the exterior of the commercial-looking building. He didn't know much about the lifestyle other than everything that happened in the club was supposedly safe, sane, and consensual. It didn't bother him if people marched to a different drum—to each their own.

As much as Tuff wanted to tell them both to fucking try getting him on a cross to be whipped, he knew, without a shred of doubt, they'd follow through with the threat. Even though he was about seven or eight years younger than them, he knew they could take him down two against one. That was the one thing that sucked about working with people trained in special ops. They could all fight dirty when they needed or wanted to. While Tuff would get in a few good shots of his own, the two men would eventually have him handcuffed, then drag him out of his house, kicking and cussing, to the Trident compound. There was no way he was letting Charlotte Roth—aka the sadistic Mistress China—get near him with one of her whips. The petite parole officer was a force to be reckoned with outside the lifestyle, so he could only imagine what she was like inside the club.

Pulling open two of the dresser drawers, he selected a clean T-shirt, boxer briefs, and a pair of cargo shorts. Might as well take a shower—a real one this time without the fucking ice—before grabbing some coffee. Either way, it was clear he was going with his boss and Sawyer, so he might as well make them wait for him to get ready.

"By the way, who picked the fucking locks on my front door?" With a regular lock on the doorknob and a deadbolt above it, the only way they could have gotten in was by picking them. He didn't bother asking how they'd bypassed his security alarm. All they'd had to do for that was tell Gordo to shut it down through her system back at BHS headquarters.

Silently but with a smirk, Sawyer pulled a lock-pick set from his back pocket and waved it in the air.

Striding to the bathroom, Tuff snorted. "Should have fucking known. Jackass."

"How many times do I have to tell you fuckers that too? Carter's the jackass." T. Carter was a US government spy under a covert agency named Deimos. He was also a good friend of the original six-man Trident team and a Dom at their club. Nice guy but definitely not someone Tuff would ever want to cross. That would be like signing his own death warrant, and as the cliché went, they'd never find his body.

Tuff shut the door behind him, then reached into the shower and turned on the water, giving it a few moments to heat up as he stripped out of his cotton shorts and underwear. Leaning against the sink, he stared at his reflection. Saying he looked like crap was a huge understatement. When was the last time he'd taken a shower? A sniff told him it had been far too long. He'd been drinking since he'd gotten home from Miami, trying to scrub the image of Kyle dying in his arms from his mind. It'd been useless because every time he began to sober up, the blood and the dying man's words came back to him. The only times he'd abstained from alcohol since then were during the wakes and funerals, but as soon as they were over, he'd gotten his drunk back on.

Stepping into the shower, he let the warm water cascade down his body and prayed it would wash those horrible images down the drain. He'd lost track of time and, honestly, had no idea what day it was. He wondered if Chet was working or not today.

Chet. Shit.

He knew he'd ignored most of her texts and messages and had seen the pity and hurt in her eyes seconds before he'd closed the door on her a few times. He didn't want to be pitied, but the hurt was his own fault. He should never have gotten involved with her.

If he'd been on the left side of the asset instead of pulling up the rear, he could've been the one hit by the bullet and died on the sidewalk in broad daylight. His job was dangerous and one of the reasons he'd always refused to get too deeply involved with a woman. Who knew when she might get that knock on the door that every spouse, girlfriend, boyfriend, or family member, who had someone in the military or law enforcement, dreaded getting? He couldn't let Chet go through that, so the best thing to do was to extract himself from her life. Maybe they could return to being just friends after a while—he didn't want to cut her out of his life completely—but it would most likely take a while for her hurt and probable anger at him to subside.

Damn, he missed her. There'd been several times during his drunken stupors over the past two and a half weeks he'd almost gone and knocked on her door, but he'd always managed to stop himself—except once. Thankfully, she'd been out at the time, and he'd ended up stumbling back into his own unit and falling asleep on the couch.

She deserved someone better than him—someone who worked a safe job and didn't fall apart when one of his coworkers died in the line of duty. Part of him knew that was irrational thinking, considering she was a sworn officer who carried a gun and enforced the state and local laws governing animals for a living. But Tuff went on missions that were far more dangerous than the one Kyle had died on. The fact he'd been killed on a routine detail just reinforced the fact Tuff could be killed just as easily someday. They hadn't done anything wrong that day—everyone had done their jobs as they were supposed to.

After reviewing all the evidence, Chase, Irv, Sherlock, and the Miami detectives had told him there was nothing anyone could have done differently. Still, Tuff hadn't been able to stop replaying the incident over and over in his mind, trying to figure out what they'd missed, what they could've done that wouldn't have resulted in Chaos being killed. But his teammates and bosses were right—they'd done exactly what they were supposed to do—but knowing that still didn't ease the guilt Tuff felt in his gut.

It looked like his pity party was over, though, and he was surprised Chase had let it go on as long as it had. It was time for Tuff to pull his ass out of the liquor bottle and rejoin the land of the living. He'd been on the other side of many an intervention after a teammate had been killed in action, but this was the first time he was on the receiving end. He was about to be put through an emotional and physical wringer, so he could return to being a functioning operative again. This is what his teammates did for each other. They kicked each other's asses when it was needed. And right now, Tuff knew he needed it.

BLACKHAWK SECURITY

CHAPTER NINETEEN

"Shit!" Tuff pressed an ice pack against his sore lip as he sat in the shade in Ian's Oasis. The man's wife, Angie, had surprised him about two years ago with the grass-covered area, complete with trees, shrubs, a koi pond, a kitchen, a commercial-sized barbecue, comfortable seating areas, a weather-proof TV, and a fire pit. It also had a misting system attached to the eaves of the two warehouses that the yard sat between to keep it cool during the sweltering summer months. The area next to the building, which now housed four huge apartments for the three Sawyer brothers and their spouses, and Ian's goddaughter, Jenn Mullins, used to be just another paved section of the compound's lot. Ian was a lucky man, and Tuff liked Angie's style. She'd planned out the entire space and hadn't overlooked a thing. It was almost like a man cave, but outdoors. Of course, the Trident women used it all the time too.

Tuff and Doug "Bullseye" Henderson sat by the fire pit, the last of the operatives hanging around after getting their asses kicked for a few hours. Nearby, Ian's trained protection dog, Beau, was lying on the grass, gnawing on a Kong toy. He had full access to the entire compound, and a small device on the lab/pit mix's collar opened doggie doors located in all the buildings and the fence separating The Covenant's building from the rest of the compound.

Now that Kat had trained four new dogs—Bravo, Delta, Sierra, and Mike, collectively known as BDSM—Beau was easing into retirement. With Devon and Kristen's baby, JD, and Angie being pregnant with her and Ian's first child, the dog now spent most of his time guarding his mistresses and the tiny human instead of the compound. The Sawyers had hired a new batch of armed security guards who used BDSM to protect the fenced-in property of nearly twenty acres. After several past missions had come back and bit them in the ass, the brothers had bought up more of the wooded acreage surrounding the industrial park that had once been the base for a drug-trafficking cartel. Ian had purchased the original compound from the government after it'd been seized during an ATF raid.

"I'm getting too old for this shit," Henderson groaned as he lifted the hem of his T-shirt and inspected his bruised ribs. After Tuff had showered and had some coffee—he hadn't been stupid enough to eat anything—Ian and Chase had driven him to Trident's headquarters, where they'd put him and a bunch of employees from both companies through their paces. North of the yard, parallel to a helipad, was an obstacle course designed after the Navy SEAL's famous O-course, although this one wasn't as large. Once everyone had completed the track filled with things to climb, swing, or crawl over or under, they'd taken a five-mile run, with loaded ruck packs on their backs, in the woods to the west of the compound. Tuff had puked up his coffee and some water along the way, which hadn't earned him any sympathy—not that he'd expected any.

Then, after all that, the *fun* had started, according to Ian, the sarcastic bastard. The operatives had been paired up for hand-to-hand combat drills, and if the two bosses thought anyone was taking it easy on their assigned partner, then they had to go up in the air with Babs. Tempest Van Buren was a retired Army chopper pilot who'd honorably earned her nickname, which was short for badass bitch. She'd saved a lot of US lives over in Afghanistan and Iraq with her talented flying skills.

The only reason she wasn't still serving in the military was that her leg had ended up being amputated below the knee after an RPG hit the bird she'd been flying. Despite her injury, she'd been able to do a hard landing, far enough away from enemy insurgents, saving the lives of the several Marines who'd been on board, as well as her own. After recovering and learning how to use her new prostheses, Babs had accepted a position with Trident. She now piloted the company's stealth Blackhawk and was the head mechanic for their fleet of vehicles. She also had a bit of a sadistic streak. Tuff had ended up pounding the shit out of Henderson since the alternative was to go on a roller-coaster ride with Babs. She loved doing all sorts of dives and loops in the chopper, and Tuff would've puked up his entire digestive system if he'd gone airborne with her.

"Sorry, dude," Tuff replied as he gently leaned back in his Adirondack chair. Everything hurt now—Henderson had given as much as he'd gotten. Tuff's hangover headache was the least of his complaints. "And you're a few years younger than me, so don't give me crap."

"Oh, my God! What happened to you two?"

The men winced at Jenn's high-pitched question, both for different reasons. Tuff's was because it stabbed his already hurting brain, but Henderson's reaction was due to something different altogether. Tuff had realized a while back that the twenty-two-year-old woman was interested in being more than just friends with Bullseye. The man was the head of Trident's Personal Protection Division, having left BHS to take the position when it'd been offered to him. The retired Marine sharpshooter had been on Jenn's security detail twice in the past when her life had been in danger and had even taken a bullet in the chest, collapsing his lung, while protecting her, hence his nickname. But being eight years older than the pretty blonde, Henderson thought she was too young and simply had a hero complex toward him.

Tuff suspected the man was denying his own attraction to Jenn, mainly because of the age difference and because she was the boss's goddaughter. She also considered the rest of Trident's original, six-man Alpha team to be her uncles, as they'd all served with her father. The men had dubbed her "Baby-girl" when she was born, and the affectionate moniker remained today. Henderson probably used it as a constant reminder to keep his distance from her, though Tuff wondered if the man was fighting a losing battle.

She sat on the edge of the fire pit, looking over their injuries—they probably appeared worse than they really were, considering nothing was broken or required stitches. Her gaze lingered on Henderson's exposed abs until the man dropped his shirt again.

"Your Uncle Ian's a sadistic slave-driver, Jenn. You should know that by now," Tuff said with a harrumph.

The young woman rolled her eyes. "Which one of you needed your butt kicked?"

Henderson threw Tuff under the bus by silently pointing at him, his eyes on the bruised knuckles of his other hand so he didn't have to look directly at Jenn.

"Thanks, buddy." Tuff shook his head, then shrugged. "Yeah, it was me, but your uncle and Chase called it a training drill."

"Of course they did." She paused, then added, "I'm sorry

about Kyle—he was a nice guy." Her tone had softened as her gaze met Tuff's in understanding. She certainly had the personality and sympathetic ear that would help with her chosen career. She was going into clinical social work and only had a few more months before she graduated with her bachelor's degree in sociology. Then she'd start on her master's degree in social work. "I know you were there when it happened. I'm sorry you had to go through that—I hope you're doing okay."

He gave her a sad but gracious smile. She really was a sweet young woman. "Thanks, Jenn. I was messed up for the past few weeks, but thanks to Ian and Chase dragging me out of bed and making sure I got my head screwed on straight again, I think I'll be okay."

He'd told her the truth. It wasn't the first time he'd lost a teammate, but he hoped to God it was the last. He had to pull himself out of the gutter and get back to work, though, and do what he did best. He'd do it for Kyle and everyone else he'd known who'd lost their lives while protecting others. It was the best way to honor their memories. "I've been ordered to spill my guts to the company shrink too, which is better than doing it in Bab's bird."

She grinned at him. "I'm glad to hear that. I only wish it hadn't taken this . . ." She gestured to his fat lip and Henderson's black eye. ". . . for you to get your ass back in the game."

"Stop cursing, Jenn," Henderson said with a growl, startling both her and Tuff.

Her eyes narrowed at him, her scowl matching his. "All I said was ass, Doug, and since it's another name for donkey, it's technically not a curse. Besides, you're not my dad, my godfather, or even my boyfriend, so you have no right to tell me what I can and can't do. I'll say whatever I damn well please." Before he could respond, she stood quickly, her back ramrod straight in defiance. "Goodbye, Tuff. I hope you feel better soon. If you'll excuse me, I have things to do."

Turning, she strode toward the parking lot without a backward glance or a goodbye to Henderson, who glared at her retreating form. If Tuff wasn't mistaken, the man's gaze was on the blonde's ass while his jaw tightened, and a tick started at his temple. Yup, Henderson had it bad. The question was, what was he going to do about it? Tuff wasn't going to ask him, though, he had his own woman problems, but it looked like Jenn was done with being ignored or treated like a child.

Shit. He owed Chet an apology and lots of groveling for being a drunken asshole the past couple of weeks. Hell, he hadn't even known she'd tried to put Meat in another foster home. Chase had been the one to tell him that and to read him the riot act for letting his guard down when Chet might be in danger. Yup, he'd fucked up. Now, he just had to figure out how to make it up to her without dragging her into his bed like a caveman. He'd just proven he wasn't good enough for her by putting his grief before her safety. She deserved someone a lot better than him. The problem was he didn't want to think of her in anyone else's arms.

He clenched his aching fists. Damn it, Henderson wasn't the only one who had it bad.

CHAPTER TWENTY

Chet threw a ball across the yard for Meat and watched the big lug race after it. Once he'd figured out how fetch was played, he loved the game. He never missed an opportunity to coax Chet into throwing the beat-up rubber ball for him.

"Hey."

Startled by the softly-spoken word, she turned to see Tuff standing on his back porch with his hands in the pockets of his jeans. His hair was wet as if he'd just taken a shower, and even though he had a slight five o'clock shadow, it was clear he'd shaved earlier in the day. He had a sheepish expression on his battered face. Chet's eyes widened in alarm when she noticed his injuries, and she rushed over to the divider separating her half of the porch from his. "Oh, my God, Tuff! What happened?"

Besides a fat, split lip, his cheek was bruised, and there was a one-inch laceration above his right eye, which was being held together by a small butterfly bandage. Pulling his hands out, he held them up. His knuckles were also split and bruised. "Relax, it's okay. We had some intensive training today. You should see the other guys."

Her brow furrowed. "Your boss and that other guy did this? It's not exactly how I expected them to help you when I saw them this morning."

"Nah, they sat on the sidelines and watched after they woke my ass up with a few buckets of water. I hope my bed is dried out by now."

"What?" Despite her worry about him, a giggle started in her chest until it turned into a full-blown laugh. "Oh, my God! I can't believe they did that!"

Tuff snorted. "I can—and believe me, I got off easy." He stepped closer and scratched Meat's head after the dog jumped up and put his paws on the railing. "Hey, Meatball, how's my buddy? Did you miss me?"

Meat groaned loudly as he leaned into Tuff's hand, letting him know he'd definitely missed him.

With a heavy sigh, Tuff's apologetic gaze met her concerned one. "Chet . . . look, I'm really sorry. I was an ass—a giant one. I'd like a chance to explain and make it up to you if you'll let me. Can we go for a ride? I thought maybe we could head to the beach. I packed a cooler with food and drinks for dinner. Meat can come with us—I've got a bone for him too."

Chet knew she shouldn't sound so eager, but she couldn't stop the "Yes! We'd love to!" from bursting from her mouth. She'd missed him something fierce and wanted nothing more than to get back on an even keel with him. She still wasn't sure where they stood—were they returning to being FWBs or just friends? Neither way was what she really wanted from him—a real relationship—but if he couldn't give her that, then, for now, she'd settle for whatever she could get because not having him in her life at all these past few weeks had really sucked.

He grinned at her. "Great. Meet you out front."

Twenty minutes later, they walked onto the dog-friendly beach they'd frequented. Off to the right, in the sand, were several picnic tables, and one was currently empty. While Chet let Meat sniff around—she still wasn't comfortable letting him off-leash yet—Tuff placed the large cooler and a wicker basket he'd brought with them on one of the table's benches. She watched in awe as he pulled a red gingham tablecloth from the basket and spread it out before placing ceramic plates, silver flatware, wine glasses, and cloth napkins on top of it. From the cooler, he retrieved two bottles of Stewart's root beer, her favorite, and several containers she knew he'd gotten from a little gourmet shop in their neighborhood. They always had a hot and cold buffet out, and customers could pick and choose what they wanted, putting it all into takeout containers that were weighed at the register. Chet often grabbed dinner there when she was late getting home from work and didn't feel like cooking or defrosting any of her frozen meals.

After the table was set, Tuff pulled out a second tablecloth and laid it on the sand in the shade of the table. "Hey, Meatball. Look what ol' Tuff's got for you, dude."

The dog stopped his inspection of a nearby dune and jogged over to where Tuff held a meaty bone in his hand. Pointing at the middle of the red and white tablecloth, he gave the German command for the dog to sit. Once Meat was in position, Tuff gave him several more commands—down, stand, speak, and quiet—in the foreign language Chet had taught him to help train the pit bull. "Braver Hund. Good dog. Here ya go, enjoy it. You earned it."

While Meat settled down on the makeshift blanket to munch on his treat, Tuff gestured for Chet to sit at the table, then sat down across from her. "I wasn't sure what you were in the mood for, so I got a little bit of everything."

He opened containers filled with pasta primavera, barbecue spare ribs, chicken marsala over rice, shrimp cocktail, steamed asparagus, and Caesar salad. Chet's eyes widened at the small feast. "Holy cow!"

"Nope, sorry, Meat got the only thing that came from a cow."

Rolling her eyes, she groaned as she reached for the salad container. "That was a lousy pun."

"Yeah, forgive me. I haven't been too witty lately." He pushed out a heavy breath. "Hell, I haven't been much of anything lately. I'm sorry, Chet. The last few weeks have been really hard on me, and because I didn't want to take it out on you, I pushed you away without much of an explanation."

"Tuff, it's okay, I—"

"No, it's not okay." He ran a hand down his bruised face, sadness filling his eyes. "Yeah, I was hurting. It's not the first time I've had a teammate shot in front of me and die in my arms, and it never gets any easier. But that's no excuse for pushing you away."

Chet gasped before he finished speaking and put down her fork. Reaching across the table, she placed her hand on his tattooed, muscular forearm. "Oh, my God. Tuff, I'm so sorry. I-I didn't know the details." All she'd known was what he'd told her that night when he canceled their plans before disappearing into his half of the house, refusing to let her console him—a teammate had died during their out-of-town mission. She hadn't even known where they'd been or what they'd been doing.

Tuff had told her a little more about what he did during a meal in her kitchen one night. His company employed mostly ex-military operatives, and some of their cases or missions were classified—as in they did some work for Uncle Sam.

She wouldn't press him for more information about the mission gone wrong, no matter how curious she was. Being in a law enforcement division, she understood that certain things couldn't be discussed with people not involved with specific cases. If Tuff could only tell her this much, she'd accept it and do what she could to comfort him.

"It's okay. I didn't expect you to know. With Chase's connections, he was able to keep Kyle's name from being released to the press." His hand covered hers, and when she looked at him, several different emotions flashed in his eyes, and it was hard to tell what they all were. Relief? Solace? Uncertainty? Lust? Well, that last one wasn't hard to figure out. She'd seen it many times before.

Chet felt a stirring in her core. Damn, she'd missed him.

His thumb brushed over her knuckles as he sighed. He seemed to be weighing his words before he spoke. "I brought you here tonight to tell you we should go back to being just friends."

Her stomach and face fell, but when she tried to pull her hand away, he tightened his grip, holding her there. "Let me finish." When she relaxed a little, he continued. "That's what I *should* tell you . . . but I can't."

Shaking his head, he bit his bottom lip before releasing it. "I fucked up, Chet. I let my grief consume me. I pushed you away and left you unguarded. I was trying to drown myself in alcohol because it hurt too much to keep reliving what happened in my head. And in the process, I was trying to convince myself the worst thing I could do was fall in love with you because you deserve so much better than me."

BLACKHAWK SECURITY

CHAPTER TWENTY-ONE

Chet's jaw dropped. This was so not going the way Tuff had planned. When he'd arrived home with the fixings for a picnic, he'd had every intention of telling her that their friends-with-benefits relationship was best brought down to a hands-off one. He'd figured at the relaxing beach, they'd be able to talk for a while, and she'd realize he still wanted to remain friends with her, and he wasn't trying to blow her off. But the moment he'd seen her standing on her back porch, he felt a slight chink in his resolve. Then she'd smiled at him, and his gut had twisted. The ride over hadn't helped at all because her nearness and her subtle perfume had driven him nearly crazy with desire.

The final blow to the armor around his heart had been when she'd laid her hand on his arm in comfort, and he'd seen the pure compassion in her eyes. For over two weeks, he'd been trying to drown his sorrows in booze when what he should have done was bury himself in her sweet body. Chet would have been beside him in bed each night and held him through his nightmares. She would have said all the right words of comfort and helped lift his spirits like he'd done when her friends had been killed. She wouldn't have pushed him away—she wasn't like many of the one-dimensional women he'd dated in the past who only wanted a good time or to change him into potential-husband material.

No, his little bomboncita was stronger than most women he knew. She was kind, caring, beautiful, passionate, and tough enough to stand up for what she believed in. She rescued animals and then fostered them, even if it meant she could be in danger. She was the most incredible woman he'd ever known, and like a fool, he'd almost thrown her away because he'd thought she couldn't deal with his job.

Ian had pulled Tuff aside earlier, after the sparring matches were over, and given him a sarcastic version of a pep talk. What it boiled down to was Tuff could get struck by a car crossing the street tomorrow or go down in a plane crash. Chet could be shot and killed in her driveway or drop dead of some medical problem she wasn't aware of. It happened to random people all the time, people who everyone else thought would live to be one hundred. There were no guarantees in life. Why should Tuff spend the rest of his alone?

He thought back to the night when he'd gone with Chase and Irv to tell Kyle's fiancée and parents he wasn't coming home. Becca had taken one look at the three men on her doorstep and had known instantly what they were going to tell her. She'd collapsed on the floor and screamed before they could even get a word out. She'd told them later she'd felt something awful had happened just around the time Kyle had been shot. It wasn't the first time Tuff had heard of a person madly in love, having that intuitive feeling that something had happened to their significant other. If something happened to him, would Chet know before she was told? Would he know if she was the one who was killed?

For once, just once, Tuff wanted to be selfish. He wanted

the woman he'd fallen in love with. He couldn't fight it anymore and hoped to God it wasn't too late.

Forgetting about the food, he stood, walked around the end of the table, never letting go of Chet's hand, and straddled the bench next to her. He brought her knuckles to his mouth and kissed them, ignoring the sting of his split lip. She still hadn't said a word, just staring at him in shock, and he wasn't sure if that was a good or bad thing. "If you'll have me, Concetta, I want more than just a friends-with-benefits thing. I can't guarantee I won't fuck up again at some point, I'm not perfect, but I do know I was even more miserable these past few weeks because I didn't let you in. I needed you, but I was so afraid you wouldn't be there for me."

"I would've been there, Tuff." She cupped his bruised cheek gently. "I wanted to be there for you so badly."

"And I shut the door in your face." He rolled his eyes. "God, I'm an ass."

She smiled. "No, you're not. You're human. We all have our faults and moments of weakness. It's when we don't learn from them that they become a hindrance."

"Well, I definitely learned something. I learned I'm in love with you, sweetheart. That's never happened to me before. Never has a woman taken up residence in my heart. But you have." He tapped the left side of his chest. "You're in here, and I don't want to let you go. Can you forgive me?"

Her smile widened as she leaned forward. She brushed her lips across the non-swollen part of his mouth. "There's nothing to forgive, Tuff. And, by the way, for the record, I love you too." She held her hand over her heart and repeated his words from just a moment ago. "You're in here, and I never want to let you go."

LYING IN BED, Tuff glanced at the clock on the nightstand next to a sleeping Chet. She was tucked into his side, her head on his shoulder. It was two a.m., and he was wide awake. On the floor next to him, Meat was snoring softly, with an occasional grunt and sigh. After returning home from their picnic, they'd left the dog in the living room with the bone he'd still been gnawing on, stripped each other bare on their way to Chet's bedroom, and drove each other crazy. For the first time in his life, Tuff finally understood what it meant to make love to a woman. With all those who'd come before her, it'd just been sex, but with her, it was so much more. She'd burrowed into his heart, and he was more than happy to have her there.

Her mom would be arriving in about twelve hours, and Tuff was looking forward to meeting Mariana Suarez. He got the impression Chet was a lot like her—sweet as candy but tough as nails when she needed to be. He was happy the woman was moving to Florida and would be close enough for Chet to see her often.

He was a little nervous, though. It'd been a long time since he'd been introduced to the mother or father of a woman he was dating. But it was more than that with Chet. They weren't just dating, at least not in his book. This was the woman he could see himself walking down the aisle with someday. He wanted to see her pregnant with his child and then grow old with her. Very old. He wanted the life Kyle was supposed to have had.

The hand on his chest caressed his skin.

"You're thinking too much," Chet murmured into the crook of his neck before nuzzling him there. "I thought you were worn out enough to sleep the whole night."

He kissed the top of her head. "Sorry, didn't mean to wake you."

Her hand slid down his torso, pushing the sheet out of the

way, and his breath hitched when it didn't stop until it reached his cock, which grew instantly at her touch. He groaned. "Chet—"

"Shush." She began kissing the same path down his chest and abdomen her hand had taken moments before, and she slowly pumped his stiff shaft. "You had your way with me earlier. Now it's my turn. Hands behind your head."

A smile spread across his face as he put his hands between his head and the pillow. "Yes, ma'am."

His leg twitched when she licked the seam where his hip and thigh met. Somehow, he kept his eyes open just enough to watch her take him into her hot mouth. His pelvis bucked in a natural reaction. "Oh, shit! Baby, that feels so good! God, yeah!"

Slowly, she bobbed her head up and down, swirling her tongue around his hard flesh. She took him deep, causing him to hiss and gasp. Her hand cupped his balls, kneading them softly. He ran a hand down her naked back and squeezed her ass cheek.

She lifted her head and frowned at him. "I told you to keep your hands behind your head."

Smirking, he pulled her leg over him and then dragged her body backward up his until she straddled his face. "Too bad, my bomboncita. I want to eat your sweet pussy while you suck my dick. First one to make the other come wins breakfast in bed in the morning."

"Hmm. You're on."

She was already soaked for him, and he ran his tongue over her swollen labia. Her spiciness coated his tongue. Chet squirmed and moaned but then went back to pleasuring him. Wrapping his arms around her hips, he held her in place and feasted on her. He was determined her climax would come before his, but, damn, if she wasn't making it difficult. Every time she sucked hard on his cock, he was one step closer to detonation.

Pulling her cheeks apart, he ran a thumb over the rosette of her anus, causing her to hum around his cock. He knew no man had ever taken her there. One of these days, he'd have to try to talk her into it. She hadn't been turned off by the idea when he'd asked her about it one night, but she also wasn't too keen on it yet. He hoped to change that someday, but if she said no, he was more than willing to fuck her mouth and pussy instead.

Chet tightened her hand around his cock, just below where her lips were suctioned around him, and she sucked in hard.

Holy fuck, I'm gonna explode.

Doubling his efforts, he whipped her clit with his tongue. Leaving one thumb at her rear entrance, he used the other to fuck her vagina. She gasped and pulled off him, coughing. He would have stopped to make sure she was okay if she wasn't rocking her hips faster and faster against his assault.

"Oh, God!" Despite being close, she took him deep into her mouth and swallowed hard several times. Tuff thought he was about to lose the bet, but then her body seized as she came for him. Seconds later, he followed her over the edge, unable to resist any longer. She swallowed every drop, then released him and collapsed on top of him, the last of her own climax waning.

Tuff kissed her clit, then grinned. "I hope you know how to make pancakes, baby."

With her head resting on his thigh, she maneuvered her body just enough, so her heavy-lidded gaze met his. "Only if you like hockey pucks, hon. Pancakes fall under baked goods in my cookbook. I suggest you go with an omelet."

He winked at her. "An omelet it is."

CHAPTER TWENTY-TWO

Tuff caught Boots nodding beside him in a mandatory defensive driving course and smirked. They had to take the stupid course every three years to keep Chase's already ridiculously high insurance rates from entering the upper stratosphere. At least it also kept Tuff's car insurance rates down too. It helped that a lot of his accidents had been on classified missions. It meant his name hadn't appeared on any paperwork filed with any insurance company for those incidents.

Tuff was tired himself, but he was sure Boots's problem was the rug rat still not sleeping through the night and not from a few hours of marathon sex with his woman. Of course, Tuff had taken great pleasure in pointing out the fact to his partner that morning, to which the response had been two middle fingers stuck up in the air, followed by, "Fuck you, asshole. Just wait until you have kids, I'm going to laugh my fucking ass off."

Usually, Tuff would have snorted and rolled his eyes because there'd been no way he would have kids anytime soon, but after last night, he couldn't get the image of him and Chet, with a few little ones of their own, raising them with lots and lots of dogs, out of his mind. Damn, they'd need a new house and a huge, fenced-in backyard.

For the first time in his life, Tuff was thinking about a long-term future that had nothing to do with job security or money for retirement and everything to do with the woman whose bed he hadn't wanted to leave that morning. He'd never told a woman he loved her before—well, he had in high school, but that was only because he'd been trying to get into the head cheerleader's panties.

After joining the Army, he'd quickly learned that once military bunnies heard those words out of the mouth of a guy in uniform, especially one in special ops, they started bringing out the bridal magazines. Now he was glad he'd never said "I love you" to another woman as an adult because he knew they weren't *just* words. Chet was the woman who'd earned them simply for being her. She'd wormed her way into his heart and soul, where she'd remain for the rest of his life, of that he was certain.

"All right, let's take a ten-minute break," announced the skinny, metrosexual guy who'd been teaching the course.

The twenty men and three women in the classroom on the second floor of the BHS building stood almost as one and headed for the door. Tuff had barely reached the hallway when his cell phone vibrated in his pocket. It was almost two p.m., and he doubted it was Chet calling him since her mother was due to arrive at the house at any moment.

Pulling the phone out of his pocket, he checked the screen and frowned, wondering why Isaac Webb was calling him.

Stepping to the side of the hall, out of traffic flow, Tuff answered the call. "Hey, Detective, what's up?"

"Hey, Tanner." Tuff's brow narrowed. The man sounded like he was in pain. "Sorry about this, but I've got bad news. Jose Martinez made bail and was cut loose yesterday."

"What the fuck?" Tuff practically yelled into the phone, causing those in the hallway to freeze and stare at him. He ignored them, striding toward his cubicle. "Why are you just telling me this now?"

"Sorry, but I was sidelined with an emergency appendectomy yesterday morning and was in surgery when the fucking ADA called and left me a goddamn message. I'd told him to keep me updated until we figured out if Martinez was connected to the Spender murders or not." He groaned and muttered another curse. "Trust me, I'm as pissed as you. He didn't bother letting my partner know he couldn't reach me. I just got my phone back from my fiancée and checked my messages. I called you right away."

Tuff wasn't surprised. The assistant district attorneys tended to rotate in for a year or two, get their experience, then move on to a better paying job in private or corporate practice. It wasn't the first time he'd heard the local cops bitch about the DA's office. But right now, he didn't give a crap about them. Martinez had been out for a full day, which meant Chet could be in danger. "Thanks. I gotta check on Chet. If you hear anything else, let me know."

"You got it."

Disconnecting the call, Tuff hit the speed dial for Chet. After the fifth ring, it went to voice mail, and Tuff cursed under his breath. "Chet, it's me. Call me as soon as you get this message. Martinez was released on bail yesterday. I'm on my way home to make sure everything's okay. Don't worry, I won't scare the hell out of your mom when I get there. Call me, baby. I-I love you."

Grabbing his keys, he spun around and stopped short. Blocking his way to the exit were his partner, Chase, and Irv. All three were staring at him in concern. The big boss was the one who asked, "What's going on? Is your woman okay?"

Shaking his head, he pushed past them, and they fell in

behind him as he strode toward the stairwell. "I don't know. That asshole from the dog fighting ring was released yesterday afternoon, and due to a series of events, I'm just finding out now. She didn't pick up her phone, so I'm heading home to make sure she's okay."

"I'm going with you," Boots said without hesitation. "Besides, it's about time I meet the woman who got you to say those three little words."

"She's hot," Chase added.

"No shit, when did you see her?" Irv chimed in. It seemed like they were all tagging along for the ride. "If she's hot, what's she doing with him?"

Tuff growled even though he knew the guys were slinging shit just to keep him from freaking out. He ran down the two flights of stairs to the underground parking lot and tried to reach Chet again as he jogged toward his truck. Again, it went to voice mail.

He tried to convince himself she was busy catching up with her mom, but he couldn't get the sinking feeling that something was wrong out of his gut. He jumped in the driver's seat of his truck as Boots took the passenger seat. Tuff cranked the engine, threw the gear shift into drive, then peeled out of the parking spot. Seconds later, Chase and Irv were on his tail in the latter's Suburban. Tuff prayed that when they got to Chet, they'd have a good laugh, and all the panicking had been for nothing. He couldn't lose her less than twenty-four hours after he'd said he loved her. The powers that be in the universe couldn't be that cruel, could they?

CHAPTER TWENTY-THREE

Going from room to room, Chet double-checked everything was neat and clean for her mother's arrival. She loved her dearly, but her mother could be a neat freak at times and would start "helping out" five minutes after she got there. Chet wanted her to relax and just enjoy her visit.

She glanced down at Meat lying on the kitchen floor, still gnawing on the giant bone Tuff had given him. She'd been surprised this morning when he'd kissed her before heading to work and told her how much he was looking forward to meeting her mother tonight. He was taking them both out to dinner. Chet was certain her mother would love Tuff once she got past the shock of his tattooed arms. It wasn't that she was against tattoos, but in Chicago, like many big cities, gang members were covered in them. Thankfully, Chet's brother, on the good side of the law, had a few now, so their mother was used to them.

Her hand went to the pocket of her capri pants, looking for her cell phone to check the time, and came up empty. "Where the hell did I put that thing now?" She was always putting it down somewhere in the house and then losing it. More than once a week, she'd have to grab the cordless house phone in the kitchen and call the cell number to find it.

Before she could go looking for it, the sound of a car pulling up to the curb in front of the house caught both Chet's and Meat's attention. Dropping his bone, he stood and barked several times.

"Ruhig, Meat. It's probably just your grandma. She's a little nervous around big dogs, but if you make a good first impression, she's gonna spoil you rotten."

As if he'd completely understood her, beyond the command to be quiet, the dog sat down, his tail wagging furiously, and lifted a paw in the air. Chet chuckled. "Yes, that will do perfectly." She rolled her eyes as she walked toward the front door, with him plodding behind her. "Jeez, I sound like Tuff having conversations with you."

When she'd teased Tuff about chatting with the dog a few weeks ago, he'd pointed out that she did it too, though she'd never really realized it before. Now, she noticed it all the time. Well, Meat was easy to talk to, and there were times like this when Chet honestly thought the dog knew exactly what she was saying.

Before she opened the door, she gave him the commands to sit and stay, then praised him when he followed them. While he was still a work in progress, he'd come a long way since she'd first rescued him.

Stepping out onto the front porch, she smiled when she saw her mother climbing out of a rental car. After closing the door to keep Meat in the house, Chet hurried down the steps. "Mom!"

Not waiting for the older woman to shut the driver's door, Chet threw her arms around her and hugged her tightly. Tears came to her eyes. It'd been almost a year since they'd been together, and it hit her how much she'd missed seeing her mother in the flesh instead of just talking to her on the phone several times a week.

"Concetta, baby. Oh, I missed you so much!" Her mother was reluctant to release her as well. They stood there in each other's arms for a minute or two. Chet had always had a very close relationship with her mother, despite living several states away.

After a few more moments, Chet patted her mom's back and pulled away. "I'm so glad you're finally here. I've planned a whole bunch of things for us to do this week, but for now, let's get your stuff inside. I'll introduce you to Meat. He's waiting patiently inside like a good boy. Don't forget, he's a pit bull with some battle scars."

"So ugly, he's cute?" her mother asked with a laugh as she opened the rear driver's side door of the sedan. Chet snorted, knowing the question wasn't meant to be cruel. It was a response she'd given her younger sister many times when Chet had brought home all sorts of stray animals, many of them worse for wear, when Mia called them ugly creatures. Even as a child, Chet had done what she could to rehab strays and find them good homes, which hadn't always been easy. To avoid having their house overrun by wayward animals of all shapes and sizes, her parents had permitted Chet to volunteer at the local animal shelter at the age of twelve. That way, she had a place where she could bring her rescues for medical treatment and baths before helping them find forever homes.

Nudging her mother out of the way, Chet reached into the back seat and grabbed a bag from a bakery. "Mmm. There better be some black and white cookies in here."

Instead of answering her, Chet's mother gasped in alarm, causing her to spin around. She froze. Pointing a very ugly black gun at Chet was Jose Martinez. She'd recognize him anywhere. She'd been there when he'd been arrested during the raid, then had seen him at his arraignment the next morning after she'd worked with the detectives to draw up the correct charges for the judge and ADA.

"Scream, and I'll shoot the old bitch," he said with a sneer.

Despite her fear, Mariana Suarez's back straightened in response to the insult, but wisely, she didn't say a word. Inwardly, Chet cursed herself. Her gun was in her dresser drawer. Unlike the officers on patrol and the detectives, she'd never felt a need to carry her weapon 24/7. There were times she did take it with her in her purse when she went out, but that usually depended on where she was going and what time of the day or night it was. Right now, she regretted not having it strapped to her hip, although, with her hands full, it was doubtful she could drop everything and draw her gun before Martinez fired off enough shots to kill them both.

"What do you want?" She knew the answer but figured she'd ask anyway.

"You've got something of mine I want back."

She tried to play dumb. "I don't know what you're talking about."

Unfortunately, Meat picked that moment to get impatient for Chet's return and started barking inside the house. Martinez smirked. "Sure you don't." He gestured up the driveway with the revolver. "Inside. Let's go."

They both hesitated, and Chet glanced around, hoping a neighbor would see what was happening and call the police. But no one was in sight, and Martinez growled. "Now! Move it."

Leaving her mother's carry-on in the car, Chet put herself between her mother and Martinez as they marched up the driveway. Something wasn't right. It hadn't occurred to her before, but why the hell was Martinez trying to recover the dogs they'd seized? It didn't make sense. With all the freaking puppy mills out there and people failing to neuter or spay their dogs, it wouldn't be too difficult for the fighting ring to replenish their dogs—a fact Chet hated but wasn't naïve about. It might take them a few months to train the dogs to attack one another, but with the pending charges against him, Martinez would be stupid to arrange fights when getting caught again would basically ensure a long prison sentence. Why was he risking everything to recover a few dogs?

Trudging up the steps behind her mother, Chet tried to figure out how the hell they could get out of this. The last thing she wanted to do was hand over Meat to this bastard, but she couldn't risk her mother's life. Inside, the dog's curious barking had turned aggressive. Chet had seen him on the couch, looking out the front window. He must have recognized Martinez and reacted. She wondered if Meat would attack him and wished she'd taught him the German word to do so. But would Martinez shoot the dog if he lunged at him? There were too many variables for what could happen in the next few minutes.

Her mother reached for the doorknob but stopped when Chet grabbed her shoulder. "No, Mom. Let me go in first. He doesn't know you."

Pushing Chet to the side, Martinez pointed the gun at her mother's head. "Go in first. If he tries to attack me, I'll shoot her. Do what you have to so I can get near him."

Again, Chet got the feeling something was off. It sounded like he wanted Meat for something other than just for his fighting skills. Opening the bakery bag she was still holding, Chet took out two large black-and-white cookies—so much for Meat's organic diet. Hopefully, she could distract him with the food so she could get his leash on him. She didn't know if she would be able to control him. It sounded like he was scratching and bouncing off the other side of the door.

She'd have to block him somehow and hope he didn't bite her in his frenzy.

If it were just her in danger, she'd let his furry ass out the door while she swung around and smacked Martinez in the head with the bag as a distraction. Meat would tear the scumbag limb from limb, and Chet would let him. But again, she couldn't risk her mother being shot.

Turning the knob, she pushed the door open a crack and blocked the dog's exit. He was barking and trying to get past her. Chet dropped her hand in front of his face, hoping he'd get distracted by the food, but the dog ignored the offering. Dropping the cookies, Chet grabbed his collar and tried to shove him back into the house. "Meat! Ruhig! Fuss!"

"What the fuck does that mean?"

"Quiet and heel," Chet responded automatically as she tried to haul Meat back into the foyer. She grabbed his leash from the table just inside the door, and after wrestling with the pissed-off dog for a moment, she finally got it on him, but he continued to bark and lunge, saliva dripping from his mouth. It was clear he was attempting to get past Chet and her mother to the threat but didn't want to hurt them. She jerked on the leash as she'd done during his training. "Ruhig, Meat! Fuss!"

He didn't ease up, and she loudly repeated the commands. This time the words seemed to get through to him. He was still growling, but the barking and lunging had eased.

Martinez shoved Chet's mother into the foyer, then closed the door behind him. From his back pocket, he pulled out a black item and tossed it to Chet. "Put it on him."

It was a nylon muzzle. *Shit*. Meat wasn't going to like this at all. He'd freaked at the vet's when she tried to put one on him. He'd been calmer without it, and after several attempts, the vet had suggested they go slowly and see how it went. Chet had been able to scratch his ears and soothe him while they'd given him a shot to mellow him out before putting him under for the surgery to remove his abscess.

Chet swallowed hard. She had no idea what would happen next, but whatever it was, it probably wouldn't be good. She eyed the keypad next to the door. There was a panic button on it if she could just get close enough. She'd forgotten all about it while trying to control Meat. That would've been the perfect time to hit it. Martinez wouldn't have known she'd done it because the alarm only went off at the monitoring center. Somehow, she would have to try and get close to that panel or the one in her bedroom. How she was going to pull that off was the big question. *Damn it.*

BLACKHAWK SECURITY

CHAPTER TWENTY-FOUR

The moment Tuff turned into the cul-de-sac, he slammed on the brakes. Just past the third driveway on the right, in front of his and Chet's house, was a tan sedan with the rear driver's side door wide open. No one was in sight. Pulling over, he threw the SUV into Park and climbed out. Boots met him at the back of the vehicle as Chase and Irv exited the Suburban and joined them.

"What's up?" Irv asked as Tuff unholstered the 9mm at the small of his back and double-checked that it was locked and loaded.

"The car in front of the house, its back door is wide open. Looks like a rental. Chet's mom is probably here, but don't see either of them."

Irv stepped to the left a few feet to eye the sedan up the street. "Could be coming back out for luggage or something."

"Or they could be in trouble. You want to wait to find out? Because I sure as fuck don't."

"Just playing devil's advocate. If the tango's here, he could've parked somewhere nearby and walked over. Think he'd be alone?"

"I have no fucking idea, but I'll take every one of them out if they touch a hair on her head." He pivoted toward his house. He had to get there and find out what was going on. He prayed to God he was misreading everything. "Let's go."

"Tuff," Chase said, stopping him in his tracks as the three other men all pulled out their weapons. The boss handed everyone a comms earpiece he must have grabbed from a go-bag in Irv's truck. "Take it easy. If this is what you think it is, shut that shit down. It's just another op."

His jaw tightened. This wasn't *just another op*. This was the woman he loved. Chase stepped toward him. "I get it . . . I do. But you know as well as I do that you've got to keep your head on straight right now. Things will go to shit if you don't. Got me?" Knowing his boss was right, Tuff nodded. "Good. Now, let's get your girl. Hopefully, we'll be laughing about this being a big mistake in a few minutes."

Tuff would have given anything to be the brunt of a few jokes when they found Chet and her mother had simply left the car door open by mistake and hadn't heard her cell phone ringing nonstop for the past ten minutes.

As the cohesive unit the four men knew how to be, having been on many missions together, they stealthily approached the house. Boots and Irv headed around the back of Tuff's unit while he and Chase headed for the front steps. Inside the house, Meat began barking, and Tuff knew without a doubt it was in aggression instead of his "I'm having fun, throw the ball again" or "I've gotta pee" barks.

He glanced at Chase and signaled they should scale Tuff's side of the porch instead of taking the stairs because they might be spotted through Chet's living room window. His boss nodded and covered Tuff as he tucked his weapon in its holster at his lower back, then grabbed hold of the banister and hauled himself up and over. As soon as his feet hit the ground, he had his gun back in his hand and aimed at Chet's front door while Chase vaulted over the banister to join him. They inched over to the large plate-glass window until Tuff could peer into Chet's living room. It was a kick to his gut. Martinez was pointing a gun at an older woman, who had to be Mrs. Suarez. Detective Webb had provided Tuff with the suspect's mug shots out of professional courtesy. It paid to have connections.

Tuff watched Chet trying to get a muzzle on Meat, who was not cooperating. She was having trouble keeping him under control while attempting to slide the device over his nose and mouth. But Meat was intent on getting to Martinez, and by the way he was growling and barking, he'd probably rip the guy apart. Tuff was more than willing to give the dog the opportunity as long as Chet and her mother didn't get hurt in the process.

Turning his head, he gave Chase a few hand signals to indicate there was one tango with a pistol and two hostages. Chase held up his non-gun hand and showed him the text he'd sent to Gordo back at headquarters, telling her to call the cops and have them respond fast without lights or sirens. The last thing they needed was to alert Martinez he no longer had a way out.

Irv's voice came through their earpieces in a barely-audible whisper. "Boss, Tuff, the backdoor's unlocked. We can enter on your signal."

"One tango with a handgun, two hostages, and a pissed-off pit bull," Tuff replied just as quietly. "He knows the German commands in case he turns on you. Try not to shoot him."

None of them wanted to harm the dog, but they all knew Meat could be in such a frenzy he wouldn't obey the commands. He could do some serious damage if he locked his jaw around one of their arms or legs—or even worse, he could lose control and go after Chet or her mother.

Tuff checked the status of the hostages one more time—Chet had somehow managed to get the muzzle over Meat's mouth and nose and was trying to secure the straps behind his ears without letting go of the leash. Squatting, Tuff crab-crawled under the window to the door and stood again. Chase was right behind him. Once they were positioned on either side of the door frame, Tuff grabbed the doorknob and gently turned, praying it wasn't locked. He let out a sigh of relief when it rotated a fraction, then nodded at Chase. Readying his weapon, the boss whispered into his comm unit, "On three."

"Hurry the fuck up!"

Meat was squirming too much, making it difficult to connect the straps behind his big head. Rage had replaced most of the fear in Chet's body—probably fueled by the frustration of trying to get the muzzle on Meat while keeping him from lunging across the room. As she'd struggled with him, they'd slowly moved into the living room with Martinez and her mother following. Their backs were to the big window overlooking the street. Chet hadn't seen anyone walk or drive by, and she had no way of knowing if any of her neighbors had noticed the still-open car door and thought it was strange enough to call the cops. Most likely not.

She glared at Martinez, still pointing the gun at her mother. "I'm trying, asshole! It's not as easy as you seem to think it is. You want to give it a fucking try?" She'd apologize to her mother later for cursing like a sailor.

"Just get it done!"

Before Chet's gaze returned to what she was doing, she could have sworn she saw a shadow move outside the window. It was probably her imagination, but a kernel of hope stirred within her. Not wanting to draw attention to the window if someone really was out there, Chet went back to securing the muzzle. When the clasps snapped together, she finally sighed, but the relief was short-lived.

Now what happens?

Meat was still growling and lunging, but he could no longer do any damage. And that wasn't exactly a good thing. Chet looked at Martinez. "Now what?"

He pushed her mother into a nearby recliner. "Stay there." The gun was now aimed at Chet. "Get him to lay down on his left side."

Her eyes narrowed in confusion, but she did as she was told. "Meat, *platz*!" She tugged on the collar and tried to get the resisting dog to lie down. "Come on, Meat. Platz!"

It took two more attempts before he finally obeyed her command. Once he was down on his belly, tension rolling off him, she nudged him onto his left side. He was panting heavily, his chest rising and falling, as he continued to let out a few growls. Chet looked up at Martinez. "Okay, he's down. Now what?"

She really had to stop asking that question because she honestly didn't want to know what was coming next.

Martinez pulled something from his back pocket and slowly moved toward them. Chet stared at the device. It looked like the microchip scanners she used at work to see if rescued strays had registered chips under their skin to identify their owners. But she didn't understand why this asshole was using one.

"What are you doing? We scanned them for chips after the raid on all the different frequencies." The individual companies that made the chips wanted to ensure their scanners had to be purchased to read their products. There were no universal devices, although some could scan several frequencies, but not all of them.

"You scanned them for ID chips—that's not what I'm looking for." He made a wide circle around behind Meat, toward his tail, as Chet kept petting the dog and using her upper body to keep him from lifting his head and getting to his feet.

With a wary eye on the dog, Martinez squatted next to Meat's hind leg, then all hell broke loose. It sounded like the front and back doors exploded, causing everyone inside, including Meat, to jump. But the dog didn't care who was coming in, he only wanted one target. He was on his feet in a flash and lunged at Martinez, who'd still been in a crouch. The dog knocked him over and went for his throat. The only thing saving the bastard from being ripped to pieces was the muzzle.

Growls and shouts filled the air as Chet dove for her mother, but the woman had already gotten down on the floor on the other side of the recliner. A gun went off, and Chet froze momentarily before frantically scanning the room. She saw Tuff's boss kick the gun out of Martinez's hand as Tuff grabbed Meat by the collar. The dog was still trying to bite the threat, his frustration growing because he couldn't. But the nails on his paws were doing some damage to Martinez's face and chest as he struggled to get out from under the enraged beast. Martinez yelled, "Get him off me! Fuck! Get him off!"

"Meat! Fuss! Fuss! Come on, boy! You did good. Now fuss!" Finally, Tuff's voice and commands got through to the dog, and he let himself be pulled off his quarry by his leash.

"Chet, are you okay?" Tuff quickly led Meat over to where she was still kneeling on the floor, and she reached out to remove the dog's muzzle. His lungs heaved, but his demeanor changed once his jaw and nose were freed. His tongue lolled out of his mouth, and his tail started wagging like crazy as she ran her hands over his head and body, searching for any wounds.

Tuff squatted down beside her and repeated his question, concern in his eyes as they roamed her face. He cupped her cheek, and she nodded. "Yes, I'm fine. He—he's not hurt, is he? The gun went off."

It was then she noticed there were two other men she didn't know with Chase and Tuff. One had a moaning Martinez on his stomach with his hands cuffed behind his back. The other man, who'd picked up the asshole's gun, nonchalantly used his finger to point at the ceiling almost directly above Chet. "The bullet went in up there. After the crime-scene techs dig it out, a little spackle and paint, and it'll be good as new."

Chet sighed in relief—not about the simple repair job but the fact that the bullet hadn't hit anyone. "Braver Hund, Meat. Braver Hund." She turned to her mother again. "Are you okay, Mom?"

She was surprised to see a smile spread across her mother's face. "I'm fine, honey. In fact, I think I can tell my cardiologist I don't need the routine stress test he scheduled at the end of the month. If I passed this one, then my ticker's just fine."

Chet and the rescuers chuckled as Tuff's boss stepped around the recliner and held out his hand. "Let me help you up, Mrs. Suarez."

She put her hand in his. "Thank you, young man."

An amused grin appeared on Chase's face as he helped Chet's mom to her feet. It probably wasn't often the forty-plus-year-old was called "young man."

"Cops are here, Chase," the taller of the other two men said as he gestured out the big window, then strode toward the front door. "I'll let them know to stand down."

Tuff helped Chet stand, then pulled her into his arms. Her head rested on his chest, and she heard his heart beating out of control—almost as fast as her own. Lifting her gaze to his, she realized he wasn't as calm as he was trying to appear. "I'm okay, Tuff. I swear. How'd you know?"

He ran his hands up and down her back. "I got a call from Detective Webb, telling me this douchebag got out on bail. When you didn't answer your phone, I got a bad feeling something was up. If there's one thing I've learned between the Army and Blackhawk, it's to pay attention to bad vibes."

"Hey, what's this?" The man who'd handcuffed Martinez was holding up the scanner.

Chet stepped out of Tuff's embrace and held out her hand for the device. "It's a microchip scanner. That's what he wanted. Meat apparently has a microchip in him that we didn't find after the raid. They all work on different frequencies. This one isn't a canine ID. He said it was something else."

"Fucking bitch," Martinez spat out.

Beside Chet, Tuff growled, then nodded at the other man. "Boots, do me a favor and haul his ass outside before I sic the dog on him—without the muzzle this time."

Boots grinned. "I'd pay to see that, but he lucked out. The cavalry's here. Keep a tight hold on Meat's leash."

Seconds later, several uniformed officers strode into the house. The next two hours were a whirlwind of activity. Tuff had insisted the paramedics be called to check out Chet and her mother, even though they'd assured him they were fine. Detectives showed up and began interviewing everyone, and the crime scene techs arrived moments later. With Chet's help, they scanned the microchip in Meat's hind leg. There were a bunch of numbers and codes on it that would have to be analyzed by someone in the CSI unit. Unfortunately, Meat now had another appointment with the vet, this time to remove the chip for evidence.

Finally, most of the house cleared out. Martinez had already been transported to central booking, the crime scene techs had processed everything, including retrieving the bullet from the ceiling, and the detectives had finished their interviews. Tuff would bring Chet and her mother down to the police station tomorrow morning to sign the official complaints. Adding kidnapping, attempted homicide—because his gun had discharged during a felony—and numerous other charges to his already pending ones concerning the fight club and drug possession, Martinez would be denied bail this time without a doubt.

Amid all the chaos, Chet's mom had found the ingredients for sugar cookies in the pantry and had proceeded to make a few batches. Chet knew it was her way of dealing with what had happened and let her do her thing. The Keurig on the counter had gotten a workout as several people had taken Chet up on her offer for a cup of coffee. Now, the only people left sitting in the kitchen munching on the cookies were Chet, Mariana, Tuff, Chase, Irv, and Boots. Meat was lying on the floor under the table, gnawing on a new bone Tuff had asked his partner to retrieve from the refrigerator next door.

After swallowing the last of his coffee, Chase stood from the table and placed his empty cup in the dishwasher. "Mariana, thank you for the cookies. They were delicious. I'm sorry we had to meet this way, but it was a pleasure—aside from the guy pointing a gun at you, of course."

Chet's mother grinned. "Thank you, Chase. Since I'll still be trying to work off this nervous energy, don't be surprised if I show up at your offices tomorrow with more baked goods."

He leaned down and kissed her cheek, causing the much

older woman to blush. "They won't go to waste, I promise you that." He turned to Chet. "If you need anything, just let Tuff know, and we'll do it. You did a great job, Chet—most people, men or women, wouldn't have been able to stay as calm as you both did. As for Meat, he's welcome to visit Blackhawk anytime if you want to use my staff as another socialization tool."

"Thanks, Chase. And thank you all for coming to our rescue. I hate to think what would've happened if you hadn't gotten here when you did."

Irv put his hand on her shoulder and squeezed. "So do we. And no thanks necessary, Mariana. I hope the rest of your visit is smooth sailing."

"From your mouth to God's ear," she replied. "Thank you, Lance. And you too, Blane." Chet's mother had insisted on calling all the men by their real first names, and none of them had asked her to do otherwise. She'd also told them to call her Mariana.

Chase squatted down and looked under the table. "*Hier*, Meat." Chet's eyebrows shot up when the dog stood and plodded over to the man with his head down and tail wagging. Chase held his hand out, palm down, letting the dog sniff him. Meat dipped his nose and rubbed it against Chase's hand, earning himself an ear scratch. "Braver Hund."

Once Tuff's boss and teammates left, Mariana stepped over to where he was leaning against the counter and placed a hand on his crossed tattooed forearms. "First, let me say thank you." When he opened his mouth to respond, she shook her head. "Let me finish. This wasn't how I expected to meet you, Jason, but I've been watching you for the past two hours. Your eyes have barely left Concetta for more than a few seconds, and you haven't let her lift a finger."

He hadn't, especially when he saw her hands start to shake when the adrenaline crash hit her. "I can still see your fear that she could have been badly hurt, but I also see how much you care about her. I don't think I could've picked a better man to fall in love with my daughter. I don't know if you've said those words to her yet, but there's no mistaking that you love her, and she loves you. All a mother wants is for her children to be happy, and I think you two make each other very happy." She patted his arms, then grinned. "Okay, now that I'm done being sappy, I'm going to lie down in the spare bedroom for a bit. I haven't had this much excitement in years. Why don't we order pizza or something low-key and go out to dinner tomorrow night?"

From behind, Chet put her arms around her mother and hugged her. "That sounds great, Mom."

"Sounds good to me, too," Tuff said before kissing Mariana on the cheek. "And, by the way, I love your daughter very much."

She winked at him. "I know you do."

Moments later, Chet and Tuff found themselves alone for the first time since he'd left her bed that morning. He reached out, pulled her into his arms, and squeezed her tightly. As she returned the hug, she felt his body quiver. Lifting her head from his chest, she looked up into his face, shocked to see tears in his eyes. "What—"

He cut her off by cupping her jaw and kissing her. At first, he was gentle, as if he were reassuring himself she was still alive and in one piece. But when she parted her lips, his tongue swept into her mouth, and the kiss took on a life of its own. Tuff clutched her hair, holding her in place as he devoured her. Chet was certain if her mother weren't just down the hallway, Tuff would've had her completely naked and been balls deep within her already.

After a minute or two, Tuff slowed down and then ended the kiss. He picked his head up and stared down at her. "I could have lost you today. You have no idea how terrified I was when we pulled up and saw the car door open and no one around. I just knew you were in danger, and I thought back to Kyle and Becca and how she'd said she felt something bad had happened right around the time he was shot. As scared as I was, it didn't feel like you were gone. I knew you needed me and were still alive. I was ready to move heaven and earth to make sure you stayed that way. I love you, baby."

"I love you too. I didn't know how, but I had this feeling you were coming to the rescue."

At some point during Tuff's speech, Meat had wandered over and was now pushing his nose between them. Tuff chuckled and petted the dog's big head. "I love you too, Meatball. You're gonna spend the rest of your furry life being spoiled rotten by me."

"*Woof!*"

CHAPTER TWENTY-FIVE

One week later...

Sitting on a chair in one of the smaller BHS conference rooms with Chase, Irv, and Detective Sonia Lovett, Tuff flipped through the thick transcripts of Martinez's interrogation. Knowing they had him dead to rights on the kidnapping charges, he'd tried to make a deal with the assistant district attorney assigned to the case. While he'd admitted to stealing back the other two dogs and vandalizing Chet's vehicle, Martinez denied having anything to do with Terry and Megan Spender's shooting deaths. The ADA didn't believe him, but Lovett and her partner, Webb, had both agreed with Tuff—the double homicides weren't part of the dog fighting ring and whatever else Martinez and his cronies were up to.

The CSI techs had been working hard on the code from the microchip, but so far, they'd been unsuccessful in cracking it. Martinez claimed he didn't know how to decipher it either. Tuff thought that was a load of bull, though. Whatever was on there had to be big with all the subterfuge, which meant if Martinez gave up the information, he'd most likely be killed for being a rat.

"I don't get it," Tuff said. "Why didn't he just shoot Meat and the other dogs, then cut out the microchips?"

Lovett leaned forward, crossing her arms on the table. "We don't know. Martinez said he had to make sure the chip was there before taking the dog with him. He was told not to kill the dogs."

"Who told him that?" Irv asked.

"He wouldn't say."

Tuff pushed the folder full of papers away from him. "Bastard doesn't know much. Don't tell me the ADA wants to make a deal with him. Martinez isn't giving you anything of value."

When Lovett hesitated, Tuff muttered a curse. As far as he was concerned, ADA Rodney Murasaki was a waste of four years of law school. "Are you kidding me? What a fucking idiot. What? Is he trying to get a rep for clearing cases?"

"Pretty much," she responded. "Martinez is getting four-to-eight years."

Chase tilted his head back and groaned. "Which means, if he's a good little boy, he'll be out in two."

"Yup." The detective stood and retrieved the file Tuff had been reading. "Don't forget, you didn't see this."

The only reason he had was that her partner owed Ian Sawyer a favor, and he'd called in the marker. Now Tuff owed Sawyer, but that was fine with both of them.

All three men got to their feet, and Tuff shook hands with Lovett. "Thanks for bringing it by. Thank Webb for me too."

"I will. His sorry ass is coming back to work tomorrow. Too bad because I was enjoying the break from him." Her grin said she was kidding. From what Tuff knew, the two detectives were one of the best teams in the bureau. "At least

I let a bunch of paperwork pile up for him. He'll be buried under it for a few days. See you around, gentlemen."

After she left, Irv asked, "How are Chet and Mariana doing?"

"Good," Tuff replied. "I meant to thank you both for making sure the press didn't hear about it." They both waved him off, not that he'd expected anything different from them, so he continued. "Mariana left for her sister-in-law's yesterday. She's heading home to Chicago on Thursday to put her house on the market so she can move to Venice permanently. Chet returned to work this morning, although she was grumbling about it. She's still training some nitwit and said he gives her a headache by talking too much."

"Sounds like my ex-wife."

Tuff's eyebrows shot up. It wasn't often Irv mentioned the woman he'd been married to briefly about ten years ago. All Tuff knew was the union had been a disaster from day one.

Snorting, Chase just shook his head and then eyed Tuff. "Tell Chet to bring Meat to the softball practice today if she wants."

"Shit," Tuff said with an eye roll. "I forgot that was this afternoon. Did you and Sawyer figure out what the winners get yet?" The game between the two security companies was this Saturday. At first, there'd been a bunch of groans about it, but there was a healthy rivalry between them, and now there were a lot of side bets and mudslinging going on.

"Yup, but you'll have to wait until Saturday to find out."

JUST AFTER 6:00 P.M., Tuff stood next to third base in the little league field at a local park as Minx was underhand pitching a softball to her partner, Jester.

"C'mon, old man," Dusty yelled from left field. "My mother can hit better than you!"

"Your mother can do something else better than him too!" Sherlock shot back from the on-deck circle before making an obscene gesture with his hands, which brought a scowl from Dusty and roars of laughter from everyone else.

Seconds later, Jester struck out. While Minx waited for the batters to swap places, the fielders shuffled around. Suddenly, there was one cat-call whistle, quickly followed by a few more. Tuff's head spun around as he tried to figure out who the guys were all looking at. Glancing over his right shoulder, he almost swallowed his tongue. Chet had arrived in grand fashion.

She wore a red sundress with white polka dots, which showed off her amazing curves and stopped just above her knees, and cute, white sandals. Her black hair was pulled up at the back of her head in some combination bun/ponytail thing. With a little bit of red lip gloss, she looked like one of the pin-up models from the 1940s or 50s—the ones almost every guy in the military or working a blue-collar job had put up in his locker. He'd never seen her in a dress before, other than the demure, black one she'd worn to one of the wakes for her friends. To say she was a knock-out was an understatement, and Tuff wanted to whisk her away from the gazes of the men he worked with.

Hanging from the crook of her arm was a picnic basket—the very one Tuff had used the day they'd gone to the beach. In her other hand, she held fast to Meat's leash. The big doofus had spotted Tuff and was trying to get over to him for a belly rub or ear scratch. Using her free hand, Chet waved at Tuff and mouthed, "hi."

"Hey, Tanner! Stop drooling over your girlfriend and get your ass back in the game!"

Minx's shout cut into his fantasy of bending Chet over

the bleachers, lifting the skirt of her dress, and fucking her from behind. Giving her a wink, he turned and faced home plate, but between pitches, his gaze kept shooting to where she was sitting with Boots's wife and kids. Tuff, Chet, and her mother had been invited to a barbecue at the other couple's house last Saturday afternoon, and the women had gotten along great.

After Sherlock hit a foul ball, Tuff took another look and eyed Chet's bare legs again. His gaze lingered longer than it should have, but he couldn't help himself. She was fucking gorgeous and all his.

"Tuff!"

His name being yelled registered a millisecond before his head exploded in pain, and he dropped to the ground. Stars filled his vision as shouts and curses reached his ears. The one that stood out the most was Chet's terrified scream. "Oh, my God! Jason!"

He groaned. Every sound was like a jackhammer to his brain. Blinking, he tried to focus on the people standing around him, but a hot, wet tongue and muzzle prevented him from seeing anything. "Meatball! Knock it off! I'm okay!" He got his arm between the two of them and tried to push the big lug out of the way.

"No, you're not," said Boots with a chuckle, clearly relieved along with everyone else that Tuff was alert. "Let the dog give you some mouth-to-mouth, just to be sure. That was some hit you took to the head, dude." Thankfully, the softball had just grazed the side of his skull—enough to knock him down but not out.

"Tuff." Chet knelt next to him and brushed her hand over where he'd gotten hit, wincing when he did the same. "Are you sure you're okay?"

Looking up at the woman he loved, he smiled. She looked like an angel, with the sunlight framing her head from behind. How he'd gotten so lucky to have her fall in love with him, he'd never know, but he was damn glad the gods of fate had sent her his way, and he'd never take her for granted. "Never been better in my life, sweetheart."

Three weeks later . . .

"MA'AM, if you don't show me your dog's rabies vaccine records, I'm going to have to arrest you and take you—"

Whoa! What? Before Leo could say anything more, which would certainly escalate the situation further, Chet stepped between her trainee and the woman he was speaking with. "What ACO Price means, Mrs. Powell, is we're trying to make sure the child your dog bit doesn't need to receive a series of unnecessary rabies shots. If you have the paperwork handy, it will save us the trouble of getting it from your vet."

"My Bitsy does *not* have rabies, I can assure you. She's very clean and gets groomed every week." The sixty-three-year-old, widowed Maritza Powell glared at them in indignation while cuddling "Bitsy," a Bichon Frise with an attitude, in her arms. Chet and Leo had gone to her house after taking a report from the mother of the five-year-old girl who the dog had bitten an hour ago at a park up the street. While the bite wasn't too bad, the skin had been broken. If the dog hadn't received a recent rabies vaccine, they would have to quarantine it for ten days. Mrs. Powell would also receive a summons for a future court date to answer charges of not having her dog properly vaccinated. Still, the ACOs would not be handcuffing her and dragging her to the police station as Leo had insinuated.

The woman was currently facing a $450 fine for having a dog deemed to be vicious since this wasn't the first time

Bitsy had attacked someone. A mail carrier had reported the dog had tried to bite her leg a few months ago but had only gotten a mouthful of polyester. If Powell could produce the rabies vaccination record, enroll the dog in a county-approved training program, and have the dog spayed and chipped, the fine would be significantly reduced. If she refused to accept the summons today, she'd be fined an additional $200. Hopefully, it wouldn't come to that, which was why Chet took over the investigation.

"I'm not implying she does have rabies, Mrs. Powell," Chet placated. "But we need official proof of that fact to satisfy the health department. If you could find the certificate for us, that would be a great help."

The woman rolled her eyes and then huffed. "Fine, I'll get it. But I'm telling you, it was that horrible child's fault. Bitsy wouldn't hurt a fly. She was just protecting me."

From a five-year-old? Oh jeez. After interviewing several people at the park, Chet knew it wasn't the little girl's fault, but she kept her mouth shut as the woman left them standing in the foyer to get the paperwork.

"What're you doing?" Leo hissed in a low voice. "You're supposed to be letting me handle the calls. I had it under control."

Chet frowned. "No, you didn't, Leo. You were about to send her into a hissy-fit—she was already halfway there—and if that happened, she'd be completely uncooperative. Haven't you ever heard the saying that you catch more flies with honey than vinegar?" Not waiting for an answer, she continued, "And I'm supposed to observe you handling calls and step in when needed—you're still in training." Not for long, though, but she wouldn't tell him that now.

Leo's training period was scheduled to be finished next week, but it wouldn't happen. Chet had already spoken to Des about it—several times. The probie ACO was not a good fit for the job—at least, not at this point. She'd found him to be overly aggressive on some calls, like today, and lax when it came to paperwork, restocking, and other mundane requirements of a day in the life of an animal control officer. He also seemed to confuse the law enforcement powers allowed to ACO with those of sworn police officers. ACOs only covered a small portion of the state's criminal procedure and penal laws compared to their patrol counterparts. There were many laws they weren't permitted to enforce, but Leo appeared to have trouble remembering that. Des was going to have to decide whether to assign a new training ACO to Leo for another six weeks or let him go and hire the next person on the eligibility list—and based on Chet's conversation with Des yesterday and the one she'd have with him at the end of this call, they were going to let Leo go and offer the position to someone else.

"But—"

"Here it is." Mrs. Powell unwittingly cut Leo off as she marched down the hallway toward them, waving a piece of paper while still holding Bitsy in her other arm.

She thrust the rabies certificate at Leo, who stood stiffly beside Chet. He took the document and read aloud the date on it. Bitsy had gotten her rabies vaccine seven months ago, so the little girl wouldn't need to undergo the elaborate treatment. Her mother would be happy to hear that.

Chet nodded at Leo, then made a slight hand motion indicating for him to hand the woman the summons he'd filled out before their arrival. All he needed to do was verify her date of birth and phone number. Once that was done, he handed Mrs. Powell's copy to her. She eyed it in confusion. "What's this?"

"A court summons," Leo explained. He didn't need coaching from Chet for that since it was the third he'd done in the last two days. "You have to appear on the date and time at the top of the form—the court's address is there too."

"But—but I gave you the vaccine certificate. Why do I have to appear in court? This is so ridiculous."

"You still have to appear before the judge to answer charges of having a vicious dog." Leo's condescending tone grated on Chet's nerves.

"Vicious!" Mrs. Powell screeched, causing the dog in her arms to start barking and growling.

As the woman got riled up again, Chet sighed, wishing she had a huge bottle of Tylenol for the headache that had started with Leo's non-stop babbling in their truck since the start of the shift and gotten worse thanks to Mrs. Powell and Bitsy.

There were four hours left in her shift before she could clock out and head home. Tuff had wanted to take her out to dinner tonight, but she hoped he'd be okay with eating in. After a long day like this one, she preferred to cuddle on the couch with him and Meat—one little happy family.

BLACKHAWK SECURITY

CHAPTER TWENTY-SIX

Tuff threw Meat's favorite Kong toy across the beach, much to the big dog's delight. "Go get it, boy!"

He glanced at his watch. Chet was due home in a half hour as long as she didn't get any late calls. It was the first evening he'd had off all week—he'd been away for two nights, and he hadn't gotten home before 10:00 p.m. since then. Tonight, after dinner, he was taking her to the BHS's indoor/outdoor shooting range. They'd gone there several times, so she could practice with him, and he could teach her some military-style shooting tactics she hadn't learned in her training.

Things had been going great between them the past few weeks. When he was home, they'd settled into a nice routine, spending most late afternoons taking Meat for walks or rides or training and playing with him, then making dinner together or getting takeout. Nights were usually spent watching TV, going to a movie or some other fun place, and then sleeping together in Chet's big bed with Meat snoring away on the floor.

When it came to sex, yeah, that was damn awesome. Chet

had a hidden adventurous and kinky side Tuff had been coaxing to the surface. Nothing hardcore or involving dominance and submission, just a little bondage, slap and tickle, and quickies where there was a chance of getting caught by someone. A trip to a local lover's lane last week had turned into a teenage boy's wet dream come true when Chet had whispered in Tuff's ear that she'd gone to dinner earlier without any underwear beneath her miniskirt. Seconds later, that skirt had been up around her waist, and he'd been buried in her scorching heat. After fucking hard and fast, they'd barely had a chance to catch their breaths before a cop car pulled up and started knocking on the steamy windows of several vehicles parked in the little out-of-the-way spot. Chet's uncontrollable giggling had resulted in Tuff becoming dislodged from her tight core.

As for everything not sexually related, that was all going well too. Chet's mom had a potential buyer for her house, gained by word of mouth after she'd returned to Chicago. One of her neighbors had relatives interested in the home. Inspections and a loan application were in the works, and hopefully, by the end of the month, they'd have a date set for the sale. Chet couldn't wait for Marianna to move down to Florida permanently. Her brother had been happy for both of them, but Chet's younger sister was, apparently, being a bitch about it, but that wasn't swaying their mother's decision to move.

Meanwhile, Meat's training was progressing nicely, to the point he'd been allowed off-leash at the beach and park during the last week. He immediately came when Tuff or Chet called him and hadn't had any run-ins with other dogs. In fact, they'd been surprised when a small terrier had challenged the pit bull one evening, and Meat had ignored him. Instead, he'd gone off and flirted with an Australian Shepard that'd caught his eye. Not that he could do anything with her

—he'd gotten snipped two weeks ago, and Tuff had treated him to an extra-large beef bone in commiseration. Now, with his "cone of shame" off, he was back to flirting with the ladies with no chance of fatherhood.

As Tuff threw another long ball, his cell phone rang. Pulling it out of his pocket, he glanced at the screen before answering it. "Hey, Irv. What's up?"

"How soon can you get here?" his supervisor asked without any preamble or explanation of where "here" was—Irv practically lived at the BHS headquarters.

Shit—so much for a relaxing dinner tonight. "Fifteen, unless we're going wheel's up. In that case, a half hour. I have to drop Meat off at the house."

"Bring him with you and make it ten."

Tuff was not surprised Meat was welcome to tag along, but he was a little taken aback by the tersely given order. "Uh, sure—on my way."

The call disconnected, and Tuff whistled loudly. "C'mon, Meatball! Gotta go to work!"

Twenty minutes later, the big dog was snoring underneath the conference table Tuff, Boots, Reaper, and Dusty were sitting around. The big bosses were behind closed doors in Chase's office, and the man's secretary, Shannon, had told the team members to wait for them in the conference room. The four were chatting and joking when Chase, Irv, Ian Sawyer, and an unfamiliar woman and another man strode into the room. If their expressions were anything to go by, this would not be good. As they all took seats around the table, Chase made the necessary introductions between his team and NCIS Agents Barbara Chan and Nathan Dobrowski.

Chase sat in his usual chair at the head of the table. An overly loud snore erupted in the brief silence when the man paused. He let out a chuckle. "That's Meat, by the way. Trust me when I say his snores are much better to deal with than his farts. I hope to God you stopped feeding him lamb, Tuff. He can clear out the entire floor after eating that shit."

As Dobrowski raised an amused eyebrow and then glanced under the table at the massive canine, Tuff smirked. "Yes, I passed your request onto Chet, and she changed his diet back to chicken." That had been an interesting few days when she'd switched his food to try a new organic brand—smelly was an understatement. There'd been nights when they'd needed to banish him from Chet's bedroom, much to Meat's annoyance. It'd been a tossup which was worse—his gastrointestinal distress or his whining outside the closed door.

With her ever-present tablet in her hands and a microphone headset on, Gordo rushed into the room. She was already tapping away on the screen before her ass hit the seat she'd chosen. The huge monitor behind Chase lit up, and numerous computer windows opened.

Without looking at the intel, the boss said, "All right, let's get to it. Tuff, the FBI coders have deciphered—sort of—the mess on the chip that was pulled out of Meat, and it's not good. Agent Chan?"

"Thank you," the female NCIS agent responded. "Ms. Gordon, please put up the first image." The computer wizard tapped her tablet, and a photo of a pretty blonde in her mid-thirties and wearing a Naval uniform came to the forefront of the big screen. "This is Lieutenant Commander Arabella DeWitt, a doctor from the Naval Medical Research Center in Bethesda, Maryland. She was one of their top scientists, working on a biodefense agent called BR7-MX, and—"

"Wait, was?" Boots asked. "Is she dead?"

"We don't know." Chan glanced around the table, her gaze landing on Irv. "She went AWOL three months ago. We haven't figured out if she went into the wind on her own or if foul play was involved."

Chase's second-in-command's jaw tightened, and he clenched his fist—actions that weren't missed by several people in the room. Dusty opened his mouth first. "Do you know her, Irv?"

The man's tone was flat as a flounder. "I went to high school with Bella. Haven't seen her since our five-year reunion."

Tuff got the impression there was more to it than the brusque explanation, but nothing else was added. Tuff looked at Chan. "What's she got to do with Meat's microchip?"

"As I was saying, Dr. DeWitt has been working on BR7-MX for three years. During a prior research study, she and two other doctors accidentally created a biochemical that could basically eat a human from the inside out over several days, similar to necrotizing fasciitis or, what the press likes to call it, flesh-eating bacteria. From what I understand, and as you can imagine, BR7-MX produces a slow, painful death, but it's faster than its natural counterpart. It would take the victim about thirty-six hours to die, and nothing can be done to stop it—at least not yet."

"What the fuck?" Reaper spat. "Who dreams up this shit?"

"Again, it was accidental. It was discovered while they were working on the formula of a nerve gas the Russians were trying to develop."

Tuff shook his head. "Okay, but I still don't understand how Meat fits into all this."

As if on cue, the pit bull let out a snort followed by a yawn before settling back down under the table. Despite the seriousness of the meeting, a few people smiled while Gordo chuckled—the woman had a huge soft spot in her heart for the dog and now kept a jar of treats in her war-room in case Tuff brought Meat in for a visit.

"At first, the FBI had no idea he *did* fit into this," Chan said. "But once the code was partially cracked, and they realized it was somehow connected to NavMeRC, they contacted us, and we were able to fill in some of the blanks. Meat—by the way, I freaking love that name—wasn't originally with the fight club he was rescued from."

An image of a couple in their mid-thirties appeared on the big screen. "Dr. DeWitt's sister, Carla, and her husband, Evert Robertson, rescued and raised pit bulls on the ranch they owned in Maryland. Meat had apparently been rescued from an abusive owner not too long ago. Carla had bonded with him and decided to keep him instead of putting him up for adoption. The same goes for the other two dogs that were stolen from their foster homes here in Tampa—they were part of the Robertsons' permanent pack.

"A little over three months ago, Dr. DeWitt's associates, Dr. Lisa Imbierowitz and Dr. Simon Czubek, who were working on the BR7-MX with her, were both killed—Dr. Imbierowitz in a hit and run, and Dr. Czubek in a home invasion, six hours later." Their photos become enlarged on the screen, along with crime scene images. "While none of us like the coincidences, there's been no evidence to link the two incidents. From what we figured out, the team had a breakthrough earlier that day, and they were on the verge of creating the antidote. After the other two doctors were killed, Dr. DeWitt put the formulas for both the BR7-MX and the nearly completed antidote onto microchips, then implanted them into the dogs for safekeeping, we presume."

"Or she could've been hiding the formula until she found a buyer for it," Ian added wryly. While he didn't say anything, it was clear Irv wasn't happy with that suggestion. Tuff guessed this wasn't the first time it had come up in conversation today.

"That's a possibility we have to consider, but at this stage, we believe it was to keep it from falling into the wrong hands."

Tuff remembered when Chet and her mother were held hostage, and something niggled his brain. "Why did they need the dogs alive?" He glanced at Boots and then Chase. "Remember? Chet told us Martinez needed Meat alive. She couldn't figure out why he didn't just shoot the dog and cut out the microchip."

Chan leaned forward and crossed her arms on the table. "About eight years ago, Dr. DeWitt was on a team that helped perfect a self-recoding microchip—a little 007 project the Navy was doing for the NSA." Meaning it was one of those things that most people would think Hollywood had made up when, in reality, it actually existed. "Once it's introduced into a live body, in this case, Meat and the other dogs, there's a reaction to the oxygen-rich blood. As long as it remains within a living, breathing body, it's fine. If it's removed, like Meat's was, the code used for the content is no longer decipherable using the original cryptogram. When all three microchips were read with the proper scanners before Meat's was removed, they would've all made sense, and the formula would be almost completely intact. Now that his chip has been removed from the oxygen-rich blood, that portion of the formula has a new cipher—one that doesn't make sense with the other two parts, which, we think, are still in the two stolen dogs."

"So, what happens if those two are removed from the dogs? I assume they end up with different ciphers, and if there's no way to get them all on the same code again, then they're useless. Wait, you said 'almost completely intact.'"

Nodding, Dobrowski said, "Right. There's a fourth

microchip out there—we believe Dr. DeWitt implanted it in herself—that would bring the others back in sync again and complete the formulas for both the agent and the antidote. She must've panicked when her coworkers were killed and thought no one would suspect the chips were in the dogs—unfortunately, she was wrong. A day or two after she implanted them, her sister and brother-in-law were murdered, the dogs were taken, and Dr. DeWitt disappeared."

Dusty let out a low whistle before asking, "Do you think she's dead after all this time or still in hiding?"

"She's of no use to anyone dead as long as she has the chip in her body," Chan responded. "Her chip would have a fail-safe that ensures that if she dies, so do both formulas. However, once her chip is linked with the others again, and the code is deciphered, her usefulness will be over."

Tuff's eyes narrowed. "But with Meat's recovered, whoever's after his chip can't complete the formula, even if they find DeWitt, right?"

"Wrong," Chase said. "With three of the four parts intact, they'd force her to recreate the rest of the formula. Intellectually, she's on a genius level—it wouldn't take much for her to complete it again."

"And once she does, she's a dead woman."

"Right."

Crap. "Do we have any idea who's behind this whole mess? I can't see the Russians hanging out with a local gang of dog fighters."

"We believe the AAB is behind it," Dowbroski said. "They learned about the formula and are willing to kill to get it."

Well, shit. The al-Ashtar Brigades was an Iran-backed terrorist group in Bahrain that received a US State Department Terrorist Designation (SDTD) in March of 2017. It was one of over two dozen currently active terrorist cells that had the potential and desire to do major damage to the United States and its European allies. If an organization was on the SDTD list, then all efforts were made to curtail its access to resources that could be used to plan and carry out terrorist attacks. If they got their hands on the BR7-MX formula, they'd undoubtedly use it in a heartbeat.

The agent continued. "We—that being the Navy, NSA, and Deimos—have been searching for Dr. DeWitt since her disappearance. She must've known she might have to go into hiding someday, given the work she does, because she's done a damn good job of staying off the radar. Her last known location was from a week after she disappeared. She crossed the border into Canada at Niagara Falls under a fake passport. After that—*poof.*"

"Getting back to the dog fighting ring . . . " Chan said. "Ms. Gordon, the next images, please." The computer geek tapped her tablet yet again, and two photos appeared. Tuff knew the subject on the left well—it was the latest mugshot of the bastard who'd attacked Chet and her mom. He'd never seen the Middle-Eastern man in the second photo before. "Jose Martinez was hired by this man—Nasser bin Sayyid—to kill the Robertsons and steal the dogs. We believe that Martinez's plans to hand over the dogs were thwarted when the police and ACOs raided his gang's fighting operation."

A few things became clear to Tuff, the primary one being Martinez must have realized that his relationship with known terrorists and assisting them in crimes against the US would result in charges of treason. Since a weapon of mass destruction was involved, he'd never see the outside of a prison for the rest of his life and would probably be shanked within days of his incarceration. Oddly, among prisoners, treason ranked up there as a despicable offense, just below child rape and abuse. Despite being incarcerated, many prisoners remained patriotic in their own way.

Even if Martinez made some sort of deal, he never would've avoided the jail time and would've eventually been outed as a traitor. As it was now, he'd be out in a few years, still breathing and with all his body parts intact.

Silence filled the room as everyone digested the facts for a few moments. Finally, Chan said, "As they've been doing for weeks now, the three agencies will continue to try to find Dr. DeWitt. We've asked numerous private contractors, Trident and Blackhawk included, to tap their resources to help. We also need to find the two missing dogs, which we hope are still in this area and are easier to find than Dr. DeWitt has been. Until we—and the terrorists—know if she's dead or not, then the possibility of BR7-MX being used to kill thousands of people is high." She glanced at Irv. "Obviously, the Navy and US government want her alive. If it turns out she ran for her own safety and that of the country, then I'm sure AWOL and any other charges will be discouraged by POTUS." She and her partner stood, signaling the end of the meeting. "Dixon, Sawyer, as I stated earlier, we'll be your contacts down here, but Assistant Director Kilmas at the NSA can be reached in DC if needed. Let us know if you need anything, and we'll keep you in the loop from our end."

She looked at Tuff. "By the way, I've instructed one of our computer techs to make it known on the Dark Web that Meat no longer has the chip implanted in him. That should keep him and Ms. Suarez safe."

He stood and shook her hand. "Thank you. You have no idea how much I appreciate that. I'll let her know and keep the confidential stuff out of it."

"Good."

Minutes later, the only people left in the room were the men from BHS and Sawyer. Meat had finally woken up and realized the object of his adoration was there. He was now sitting next to Sawyer, staring at the man whose earlier stoic expression had spread into one of amusement. He pulled out the pouch of dog treats from his side-thigh pocket and, after a few commands and responses, handed one over.

Chase laughed. "I'm going to tell Beau you're cheating on him and giving another dog his treats."

"Beau gets plenty of them from my wife. Trust me, that dog is spoiled rotten now, thanks to her." He gave Meat an ear scratch, which was met with a loud groan of ecstasy.

The BHS boss snorted, then addressed Tuff and his teammates. "First thing in the morning, you four are assigned to tracking down the two missing dogs. If you need anything and Gordo's busy, call Cooke or Evans over at Trident." He got to his feet and glanced at Sawyer and then Irv. "Whose turn is it to buy dinner?"

Sawyer raised his hand as he stood. "Mine. Angie's got a few girlfriends over, fussing over what else we need for the baby's room—as if there isn't an entire baby store in there already."

As the three men began to file out of the conference room, Meat tried to follow Sawyer, but the man stopped and gave the command to stay. The dog wasn't happy about it, but he did as he was told with a low whine. Tuff shook his head as he stood and said, "See you guys in the morning. C'mon, Meatball—let's get home to your momma. She'll spoil you plenty too."

BLACKHAWK SECURITY

CHAPTER TWENTY-SEVEN

Chet's gut clenched when she pulled into her driveway and saw a BMW parked in Tuff's spot. Standing on the porch in front of her door was the last person she wanted to see today, if ever. Her shitty day had just gotten shittier.

Damn it. How the hell had her ex-husband found out where she was living? Actually, it probably hadn't been that hard. She was sure mutual friends talked, whether innocently or not, and eventually, someone had probably told him. If not, Roland could have easily used his brother's status as the mayor of St. Petersburg to find out. Chet's address was on file with the City of Tampa's payroll department and had been listed in the recent police reports on her vandalized car and the incident with Martinez.

She'd hoped to find Tuff and Meat home already after the day she'd had. Leo had bitched and moaned for the rest of the shift about her interference on the call with Mrs. Powell. Before Chet could take him back to the ACO headquarters, Des had texted her to say he needed to leave work early after his sister had called. Their elderly mother had fallen and been taken to the hospital. He'd postponed the meeting with

Leo until tomorrow morning, which meant Chet had needed to finish the shift with the probationary ACO. At least Des's mother hadn't been seriously injured—she'd just broken her wrist.

Now, to top everything off, Chet had to deal with her ex-husband. Unfortunately, Roland had seen her pull in, so it would be childish for her to back up and drive away. It was probably a good thing Tuff and Meat weren't here. Maybe she could get rid of him before they got home.

Putting the SUV in Park, Chet shut off the engine, grabbed her purse, and opened the door. Roland was already on his way down the steps. His movements were slow and uncoordinated, and she knew instantly he'd been drinking.

Shit.

"Where the hell have you been?" he slurred.

"What are you doing here, Roland?"

"Looking for my wife." He glared at her with watery, bloodshot eyes. His shirt and dress pants were disheveled. Either he'd been drinking in his office—he'd had a wet bar installed shortly after they'd been married—or he'd enjoyed a liquid lunch at one of the upscale restaurants he frequented.

She took several steps back as he advanced toward her. Reaching around to her lower back, she reassured herself that her gun was there but didn't pull it out. It was still daylight, and she could hear some of the neighborhood kids playing in one of the cul-de-sac's backyards. "I'm no longer your wife, and you're violating the order of protection."

A snort escaped him before his mouth turned up in a sneer. How she'd ever thought the man was handsome was beyond her. He was downright ugly, especially when he was drunk.

As she took another step back, Chet tripped on the driveway's edge where it met the lawn. Roland reached out and grabbed her upper arm, preventing her fall but digging his fingers into her flesh until she cried out in pain.

Spittle flew from his mouth as he snarled, "Fuck the order of protection. You're my wife, damn it, and I'll fuck my wife anytime I want."

What? Oh, hell, no!

As he pulled her toward him, Chet regained her balance and didn't hesitate as she brought her knee up fast and hard. Roland howled in pain and dropped to the ground in a fetal position. "You bitch! Ohhhh, God, you fucking bitch!"

Before Chet could do anything else, screeching tires caught her attention, and she turned to see Tuff parking his truck behind both vehicles in the driveway. He leaped from the driver's seat and rushed to her side, glaring at Roland, who was still in agony on the ground. In Tuff's truck, Meat was going ballistic, barking and trying to get through the closed window.

"Chet! Are you okay?"

She let Tuff pull her into his arms, noticing her limbs were now shaking from the adrenaline. "Y-yes. I'm fine."

"Good. I was pulling up and saw him grab you—holy shit, baby. Remind me never to piss you off. You dropped him like a ton of bricks."

"You fucking cunt!"

Tuff froze at Roland's shout, and Chet looked up at his face. *Uh-oh. This isn't going to be good.*

As he started to pull away from her, she grabbed his arms. "Tuff, don't. Please."

He ignored her plea, rage flaring in his eyes. Reaching down, he grabbed her ex-husband by the hair, eliciting another scream of pain. Then Tuff did something that confused Chet—he pointed his key fob at his truck. To her amazement, the windows rolled down. As soon as he could, Meat leaped through the opening of the front passenger window before charging forward. She was about to lunge for him and order him to halt, but Tuff beat her to it. "Platz!"

Meat stopped in his tracks, still barking like mad, but didn't lay down like he was supposed to. At least he'd learned the more important part of the command. In Tuff's grasp, Roland was desperately trying to get to his feet and away from both the pissed-off man holding him and the equally pissed-off dog. Leaning down, Tuff got in the other man's face. "Give me a reason—one fucking reason for me to give him the command to tear you from limb to limb."

Roland struggled against the hold. "Ge-get off me! Keep him away from me!"

"One reason, asshole!" Tuff shook him like a wet rag. "C'mon! Or are you too chicken-shit to pick on someone your own size?"

Using his free hand, Tuff grabbed Roland's shirt and hauled him upright before shoving him against the side of Chet's SUV. "If I ever see you within a hundred yards of Chet, I'll beat the living crap out of you, then order my dog to piss on whatever's left of you. Got it?" When he didn't get an answer, Tuff shook him again. "Fucking answer me, dickhead—do you understand what I'm telling you?"

"Yeah . . . yeah! All right. I'll leave—leave her alone."

Tuff tossed Roland back to the ground again as two police cars pulled up. Chet's eyes narrowed as she wondered which neighbor had called them, but Tuff turned to her and said, "I was on the phone with Brody Evans at Trident when I pulled into the cul-de-sac. I told him to send the cops over before I got out of my truck. With them on their way, I wouldn't be tempted to kill the bastard and hide his body."

The two officers obviously knew Tuff because, when they approached, they greeted him with smiles and handshakes. Within fifteen minutes, Roland was handcuffed and in the back of one of the patrol cars on his way to booking for a violation of the OP and public intoxication. The only reason they couldn't add on a DUI charge was no one present had seen him in the driver's seat of his BMW.

As a tow truck arrived to haul Roland's pride and joy out of the driveway, Tuff gave Chet a swift kiss on the mouth. "Take Meat inside and feed him—he's had an eventful day too. I'll be there in a few minutes. We can reheat the leftovers from last night. Sound good?"

She hugged him around the waist, resting her head on his hard chest for a moment. "It sounds fantastic." Chet was about to walk toward the stairs with Meat's leash in her hand when a thought occurred to her. "Hey, Tuff? What's with the windows on your truck?"

He smirked. "A new little gadget I had the BHS mechanics put in—it's the same thing the K9 officers have in their vehicles. A push of the button on the fob and the windows roll down. I figured with Meat in my truck a lot, it might come in handy—guess I was right. Cool, huh?"

"Very. I might have to have that installed in my SUV."

"I'll ask when I can bring it in—the guys will have it done in about an hour."

"Great, but I insist on paying for it." She'd figured out that Tuff told little white lies sometimes when it came to buying her things, not that it upset her. It made her feel special that he constantly ensured she was safe without suffocating her.

Cupping her chin, he leaned down and kissed her again. "I'll pay them, and then you can pay me by doing another striptease like you did the other night. Baby, that was hot as hell."

She brushed her lips across his. Damn, she loved this man. "You got yourself a deal."

BLACKHAWK SECURITY

CHAPTER TWENTY-EIGHT

Chet perched on one of the two chairs in Des's office, waiting for her boss and Leo to come in. She was so not looking forward to this conversation. Still, as the training ACO, she needed to be present as Des reviewed her evaluation sheets of Leo's performance during the past several weeks. Hopefully, within the hour, she'd be in her assigned vehicle in blessed silence. It would be a week or so before she had a new probie riding with her. With any luck, they'd be as quiet as a mouse.

Her mind flashed to two hours ago when she'd been lying in bed with Tuff. He'd shocked the hell out of her when he'd suggested they move in together.

"Penny for your thoughts?" Chet asked, snuggling into his side as her fingers traced one of the tattoos on his bare chest. She had twenty minutes before she had to get up and jump in the shower, and that was the last thing she wanted to do. She'd give anything to stay in bed, wrapped up in the arms of the man she loved.

"They're worth more than that."

She giggled. "Okay, how about a buck?"

Chet felt rather than heard him snort. "Um . . . I was just wondering . . . how averse would your mom be to us moving in together?"

"What?" She quickly sat upright, her stunned gaze meeting his apprehensive one. *"Are you serious?"*

His eyebrows raised. *"Too soon? I love you, baby."* He cupped her cheek, and she nuzzled his palm. *"I never thought I'd ever meet someone who would wrangle my heart and make me want things I never knew I was missing. Someday, I'd love to put a ring on your finger and a baby in your womb, but I think the first step should be making sure I don't drive you crazy with any habits I've developed."*

"What kind of habits?" she asked with narrowed eyes.

A devilish smile spread across his handsome face. "Well, stuff like I love to eat your pussy any chance I get and give you as many orgasms as possible on a regular basis. I'll want you naked and in my bed all the time. I'll spoil your dog with bones from the butcher."

"I noticed you called him your *dog last night when you were threatening Roland."*

His eyes danced in amusement. "Oh, that wasn't a threat, sweetheart. That was a promise. Just make sure Meat's rabies vaccination stays up to date so he doesn't have to be quarantined after making hamburger out of the jackass." He paused as she laughed, then said, *"So, you didn't answer my question. Will you move in with me, and how pissed will your mom be if you do? You know, so that I know how much I have to butter her up."*

"My mom loves you. I don't think she'll have any problem with us moving in together."

"And what about you? Do you have any problem with it?"

"Not at all. I do have one question, though?"

He rolled her onto her back and crawled on top of her, his morning erection nestled between her widespread thighs. *"And what's that?"*

"Mmm. Well, now I have two questions—the first is, which side of the house will we live in, mine or yours?"

"Yours. I like how you decorated it. It's homey versus my bachelor pad." He flexed his hips. "What's the second question?"

"How many times can you make me scream your name in the next seventeen minutes?"

His grin widened as far as it would go. "I don't know—let's find out."

Chet felt her cheeks warm as she remembered how many times she'd, indeed, screamed his name. The man knew how to make her body sing.

Glancing at the clock on the wall, she wondered if he'd make any progress today on finding the other two pit bulls that'd gone missing. While he'd said he couldn't tell her everything about what was going on, he did say they were doing everything possible to find the dogs and the microchips that'd been implanted in them. She was curious as hell but knew he would have told her if he could.

Des strode in, with Leo on his heels, then shut the door behind them. "Have a seat, Leo."

"What's going on?" the younger man asked. Like Chet, he was already in his uniform, but unlike her, he was minus his duty belt with its holstered weapon—he must have gotten dressed before Des found him in the men's locker room. Meanwhile, Des was wearing his usual uniform pants and a white polo with the ACO department logo on it.

Chet's supervisor sat behind his desk with Leo's employee file in front of him. "Leo, over the past weeks, Chet has been evaluating you. She's taught you what you need to learn, reviewed protocols and procedures, and given you numerous opportunities to gain experience. She and I have had many conversations about your progress, and I've had several meetings with you as well. I'm sorry to say I don't think you're cut out for this job. You seem to think you have more authority than the ACOs are allowed, despite Chet's and my intervention and guidance. I agree with Chet's recommendation to let you go."

"What? You can't do that!"

Biting her tongue, Chet barely stopped the words "yes, he can" from escaping her mouth. Leo glared at her before turning his attention back to Des. "But—but I still have a week left on probation. I can do it. Let me prove to you I can do the job.

"I'm sorry, Leo. You're just not cut out for this department. Maybe the police department would be a better fit."

Chet almost rolled her eyes. She doubted the police department wanted a loose cannon any more than she or Des did.

Leo slammed his fist on Des's desk, startling Chet. "No! They wouldn't take me! Please, give me a chance! All—all I need is a chance. I can do it!"

Chet's eyes narrowed, and she frowned at Leo's declaration that the police department wouldn't take him. She didn't remember any TPD application, submitted or denied, being in his file, and from a similar look on Des's face, he didn't either.

Des shook his head. "I'm sorry, Leo. We gave you several chances, but each time, you ignored our constructive criticism."

Standing quickly, his chair shoved back a foot, a red-faced Leo turned on Chet and pointed a finger at her. Rage flared in his eyes. "You bitch! You didn't like me from the first day! You were looking for a reason to get rid of me. I told Uncle Robert you'd do something like this!"

"Who?" She had no idea who his uncle was. Not wanting to be at a disadvantage, Chet got to her feet as Des also stood and came around from behind the desk.

"Don't give me that crap. You know him. Hell, you were

fucking married to his brother! Roland told me all about you being a cunt to him!"

What? "Y-you're related to Robert Stratford?"

He sneered. "Don't act like you didn't know my mother's sister is his wife. You found out, and to get back at Roland, you're getting me fired. You bitch! Do you know what I did to get this job? I should've killed you instead of that asshole and his wife!"

Before she could react to his outburst, Leo reached into his back waistband and pulled out a gun. Des lunged forward to grab the weapon, but it discharged. He grunted in pain as red bloomed on his shirt just below his right shoulder.

Her heart pounding, Chet drew her 9mm and fired, controlling the recoil with muscle memory. The bullet slammed into Leo's chest but didn't stop him as he swung his weapon toward her. Chet fired again ... and again, Tuff's voice in her ear telling her to keep shooting until the threat was down and not getting back up. It took four bullets to the upper torso before Leo dropped to the ground, never getting another shot off.

Chet stared at his body in shock, then Tuff's voice was in her head again. She stepped forward and kicked the gun from where it landed near Leo's hand, sending it skittering across the floor. She thought he was dead—hoped so—but there was no way she was taking any chances.

The acrid smell of both gunpowder and blood filled the air of the small office. After holstering her weapon and grabbing a first aid kit that hung on the wall, Chet rushed over to where Des was leaning against the desk, his hand over his wound. "Are you okay? Sit in the chair."

She steered him to the closest seat, then quickly found packages of gauze and ripped several of them open. With shaking hands, she covered the bullet's entrance and exit wounds. The projectile had gone straight through, making a larger hole in his back. Aside from being in obvious agony, his breathing didn't seem labored, nor did it appear he was losing excessive amounts of blood. Hopefully, that meant the bullet hadn't hit any major vessels or his lung.

"Lean back against the chair and put pressure on both wounds while I call it in."

After Des gingerly did as he was told, his hand replacing hers again, Chet snatched one of the TPD radios from a row of chargers on a shelf near the door. She turned it on and made certain it was on the correct emergency channel before squeezing the transmit button. "ACO-7 to headquarters, shots fired at our station. I repeat, shots fired at our station. Suspect down and my supervisor's been hit."

A female dispatcher's response was immediate. "All units, all units, clear the air—emergency traffic only. Headquarters to ACO-7, confirm you have shots fired at ACO headquarters, suspect down, one other victim."

"That's affirmative." Chet returned to Leo's still body and checked for a carotid pulse but found none. His unseeing gaze was directed at the ceiling. "ACO-1 is conscious and stable but was hit in the shoulder. We need a bus ASAP, and a patrol supervisor and detectives to respond."

"Copy that, ACO-7. EMS is on their way. Headquarters to . . ."

While the dispatcher alerted the appropriate units to respond, Chet checked on Des again. "How're you doing?"

"I'll live," he replied. Chet rolled her eyes at his dry humor. "Nice shooting." He grimaced. "And no offense, but I think I'll assign the next probie to McGregor, no matter how much he bitches."

Chet shook her head. "You won't get any arguments from me, boss."

EPILOGUE

"Thanks for coming by and checking on me," Chet said to Chase and Irv as they stood in her living room, preparing to leave. She was sitting on the couch, cuddled up under a blanket, with Meat's head resting on her lap. Although she was still stunned by yesterday's incident and Leo's confession that he'd killed Terry and Megan, she actually felt calm and relaxed today—it was still all so surreal. Tomorrow she'd have her first session with the police department's shrink, as required by the city for any officer involved in a shooting. She wasn't looking forward to telling the story yet again but knew it was necessary. She had no doubt she was going to have nightmares and PTSD on some level in the weeks to come.

As soon as the medics had taken over Des's care, Chet had called Tuff to tell him what'd happened and that she was unharmed. With all his and BHS's police department contacts, she wanted to ensure he heard it from her first, not wanting him to worry unnecessarily. He'd dropped everything and raced to the ACO headquarters to see for himself that she was okay. Then he'd stayed with her as she'd repeated her story of what had happened several times, both at the scene and later again at the detective bureau with Isaac Webb and Sonia Lovett and two officers from Internal Affairs.

After the interviews were over, and Chet had been reassured Des was resting comfortably in a hospital room, Tuff had taken her home and slept with his arms around her all night. He'd made breakfast in bed for her this morning since she could sleep in. She had the next few days off until the investigators concluded the shooting had been justified. It was a no-brainer, in her opinion, but like any other officer-involved shooting in the city, the detectives had to make sure everything was done by the book.

Detective Webb had stopped by two hours ago and filled her and Tuff in on what they'd learned since last night. Leo Price had, indeed, been Robert Stratford's nephew by marriage. The few times Chet had met Leo's parents at family functions, their son hadn't been around. TPD Internal Affairs was investigating how Leo's police department application file, which would show why he hadn't been hired, had disappeared from the city's records bureau. Chet suspected Robert or Roland had paid a cop or clerk to steal the file. If it'd been available to Des when he'd been going through the list of potential hires, Leo would probably have been passed over immediately, despite having the highest score on the list. Detective Webb believed the records would show Leo had failed the psychological exam.

A search of Leo's apartment had revealed evidence he'd stalked at least three of the city's ACOs for about two weeks. He'd waited for an opportunity to kill one of them, so a position would open up in the department where it took years for someone to retire. It was the next best thing to being a patrol officer in the city—he still got to carry a weapon and a shield. The press was having a field day already after his connections to the mayor of St. Petersburg and his prominent-businessman brother were discovered. Of course, that meant Roland's arrest two days ago had also hit the news. Both men's public relations people would be working some serious overtime in the upcoming weeks.

Chase leaned down and kissed Chet on the cheek. "No problem, Trouble. Glad to see you're okay."

She laughed at the nickname he'd given her when he'd first arrived a half hour ago. After Irv also gave her a quick kiss, the two men said goodbye to Tuff and Meat before taking their leave.

Running his fingers through his hair, Tuff sat on her heavy wooden coffee table and took her hand. "Are you sure you're okay?"

She brought his fingers to her lips. "I'm fine, I swear."

"You know, in the beginning, I kept telling myself I should stay away from you because my job can be dangerous at times, but damn, woman, I'm starting to think my job's a piece of cake compared to your daily life."

"I hope you don't think I'm too much trouble now."

Dropping to his knees, he leaned in, his mouth taking possession of hers, and Chet melted. After a moment, Tuff ended the kiss with a peck on her nose. "To be honest, you're my kind of trouble. Hot as hell in dresses and heels, yet tough enough to hold your own. I'm proud of you, sweetheart. Just do me a favor, please? Stop giving me heart attacks for a while?"

From her lap, Meat seemed to groan in agreement. A smile spread across Chet's face. "You both have a deal."

IF YOU'RE a fan of the Trident Security series and its spinoffs and are following the best reading order on my website, up next is the *Trident Security Field Manual.* It's a supplement to the series with lots of fun things such as character profiles, a Q&A, short stories, and family trees.

IF YOU WANT to continue with the Blackhawk Security series, *Blood Bound* is now available. Keep reading for a preview.

PREVIEW OF BLOOD BOUND

Using the mirror in the bathroom attached to his office, Chase Dixon made sure his burgundy tie was straight under the navy-blue suit he'd changed into a few minutes ago. The custom-made jacket and pants fit his six-foot-three, sinewy frame perfectly. It was rare for him to be so formally dressed at work—usually, he was in cargo pants, combat boots, or rubber-soled shoes, and a polo or T-shirt with the logo for his company, Blackhawk Security. But today was a big day—a very special day. One he'd been waiting a year for.

After double-checking his jawline and upper lip for any stubble that might have been missed, he silently declared this was as good as he was going to get. His aftershave was still making his skin tingle. He'd stopped at his regular barber on the way to work for a shave and to make sure his salt-and-pepper hair was nice and trim. He wanted to make a good impression when he arrived for his lunch date.

It was a beautiful March day outside in St. Petersburg, Florida—sunny but not too hot—and that was perfect weather for the occasion.

Stepping back into his office, he strode over to his desk

where he locked away his handgun, which was normally on his hip, in the top drawer. He wouldn't need it today and always had several weapons available in his truck for emergencies. If they were too far away when he needed one, his special-ops training had taught him how to use normal, everyday items to defend himself if necessary.

Grabbing his cell phone, wallet, and keys, he put each in its appropriate pocket. The last thing he picked up was the bouquet of two dozen long-stem, pink roses—he'd done a discreet inquiry and found out it was his date's favorite color.

After a quick glance around to make certain he hadn't forgotten anything, he headed for the closed door that led to the reception area. Opening it, he almost tripped over a massive beast lying on the floor, blocking his exit. Chase grabbed the jamb to keep from tumbling to the ground. "Meat! Damn it, dog, I love ya, but one of these days, you're going to send me to the freaking emergency room. If that happens, it's coming out of Tuff's pay."

The brawny, tan-and-white pit bull was a frequent visitor to the security company's headquarters. In fact, he'd been there all week since his owners, Jason "Tuff" Tanner, one of Chase's operatives, and his girlfriend, Concetta "Chet" Sanchez, were away on vacation and due back tomorrow. Bianca "Gordo" Gordon, BHS's resident computer hacker, was dog-sitting for them and had brought Meat to work with her each day. The big mush had made himself at home, wandering around and plopping down for a nap wherever he felt like it. The former rescue was now a hero after he'd helped save Chet and her mother from a gang member with a gun, and was welcome anytime at BHS—as long as he didn't have any lamb for breakfast. His farts could clear out the entire floor when he ate that stuff.

"Whoa, boss! Check you out. Damn, who knew you

cleaned up that well?" Gordo whistled, then grinned as she looked him up and down from where she stood in front of the reception desk, which was manned by Shannon Daly, the woman who kept the office running smoothly. "Who are the roses for?"

Side-stepping Meat, who'd sat up looking for a treat or an ear scratch—Chase gave him the latter—he responded, "Not that it's any of your business, but I have a date. Irv's in charge for the rest of the day."

"A date? A Tuesday lunch date with, what . . . two dozen roses?" She raised her eyebrows at Shannon, hoping the middle-aged woman would provide a few more details. "So, who is she?"

His petite, brown-haired receptionist shook her head. "Don't look at me."

"You don't know who his date is with?" Gordo's incredulous tone said she didn't believe it for a second.

"I didn't say that. Of course, I know, but I'm not at liberty to discuss it, and I like my job too much to say anything more."

Chase chuckled. Short of committing espionage, embezzlement, or murder, Shannon's employment was pretty much guaranteed until she decided to retire. He also hoped that wouldn't happen until he, himself, was ready to retire. The woman was a godsend, and the place would probably fall apart without her. He also knew his secrets were safe with her—at least the ones he was willing to share with her. In his business, there were a lot of things he couldn't talk about with anybody who wasn't directly involved.

Lance Irving, Chase's second-in-command, exited his own office, and Gordo glared at him. "Let me guess, you know who his date is with, and you're not telling either."

Snorting, Irv handed Shannon a file. "How long have you known me, Gordo?"

The computer geek sighed and rolled her eyes. "Long enough to know you're tight-lipped too."

A lightbulb seemed to go off in her intelligent mind as her eyes lit up, and she stood a little straighter, but Chase held up his hand, cutting off the idea he knew had just popped into her head. "Don't even bother. The information isn't on my schedule, so don't go through the backdoor again to snoop around. And if I find out you hacked into my phones or tracked me, there will be hell to pay."

"Shit, you're no fun when you're dressed like a hottie. C'mon, Meat. Let's go." The pit bull happily followed her into the hallway as she stomped back to her war-room.

Shaking his head, Chase turned to Irv. "Anything I need to know about before I leave?"

"Nope. Everything's covered. Have a good time."

"Thanks. Shannon—"

"I know," she interrupted. "Hold all your calls for the rest of the day. Now get out of here and have fun." She gave him a wink and then shooed him away with her hands.

Taking a deep breath, he let it out and then started for the elevator that would take him to the underground parking garage. As he waited for the sliding doors to open, he checked his watch. He was actually running early, but that was fine. The last thing he wanted was to be late and disappoint his date—she was far too special for that.

Now Available - *Blood Bound*

Right place, right time.

When Rylie Hart adopts her best friend's daughter, in the wake of the woman's untimely death, she goes from being an honorary aunt to a mother in the blink of an eye. Two years later, after kindergartner Mickey is diagnosed with leukemia, an anonymous donor is her only hope.

Retired Marine Raider and current Blackhawk Security CEO, Chase Dixon finds himself in a position to give someone the gift of life. Twelve months later, he gets to meet the little girl he saved, and not only does she instantly steal his heart, but so does her mother.

After Rylie receives legal documents contesting Mickey's adoption, she discovers the secret her friend took to the grave. Once again, she finds herself fighting for her daughter's life. Will Chase be able to come to their rescue one more time? Or will Rylie lose her little girl and the man she's falling in love with?

Also by Samantha Cole

***Denotes titles/series that are only available on select digital sites. Paperbacks and audiobooks are available on most book sites.

The Trident Security Series

Leather & Lace

His Angel

Waiting For Him

Not Negotiable: A Novella

Topping The Alpha

Watching From the Shadows

Whiskey Tribute: A Novella

Tickle His Fancy

No Way in Hell: A Steel Corp/Trident Security Crossover (co-authored with J.B. Havens)

Absolving His Sins

Option Number Three: A Novella

Salvaging His Soul

Trident Security Field Manual

Torn In Half: A Novella

***Heels, Rhymes, & Nursery Crimes Series

(WITH 13 OTHER AUTHORS)
Jack Be Nimble: A Trident Security-Related Short Story

***THE DEIMOS SERIES
Handling Haven: Special Forces: Operation Alpha
Cheating the Devil: Special Forces: Operation Alpha

THE TRIDENT SECURITY OMEGA TEAM SERIES
Mountain of Evil
A Dead Man's Pulse
Forty Days & One Knight

THE DOMS OF THE COVENANT SERIES
Double Down & Dirty
Entertaining Distraction
Knot a Chance

THE BLACKHAWK SECURITY SERIES
Tuff Enough
Blood Bound

MASTER KEY SERIES
Master Key Resort
Master Cordell

HAZARD FALLS SERIES
Don't Fight It
Don't Shoot the Messenger

THE MALONE BROTHERS SERIES
Her Secret

Her Sleuth

LARGO RIDGE SERIES
Cold Feet

***ANTELOPE ROCK SERIES
(CO-AUTHORED WITH J.B. HAVENS)
Wannabe in Wyoming
Wistful in Wyoming

AWARD-WINNING STANDALONE BOOKS
The Road to Solace
Scattered Moments in Time: A Collection of Short Stories & More

***THE BID ON LOVE SERIES
(WITH 7 OTHER AUTHORS!)
Going, Going, Gone: Book 2

***THE COLLECTIVE: SEASON TWO
(WITH 7 OTHER AUTHORS!)
Angst: Book 7

***SPECIAL COLLECTIONS
Trident Security Series: Volume I
Trident Security Series: Volume II
Trident Security Series: Volume III
Trident Security Series: Volume IV
Trident Security Series: Volume V
Trident Security Series: Volume VI

About Samantha Cole

USA Today Bestselling Author and Award-Winning Author Samantha Cole is a retired policewoman and former paramedic. Using her life experiences and training, she strives to find the perfect mix of suspense and romance for her readers to enjoy.

Awards:

Wannabe in Wyoming (co-authored by J.B. Havens) won the bronze medal in the 2021 Readers' Favorite Awards in the General Romance category.

Scattered Moments in Time, won the gold medal in the 2020 Readers' Favorite Awards in the Fiction Anthology category.

The Road to Solace (formerly *The Friar*), won the silver medal in the 2017 Readers' Favorite Awards in the Contemporary Romance category.

Samantha has over thirty-five books published throughout several different series as well as a few standalone novels. A full list can be found on her website.

Sexy Six-Pack's Sirens Group on Facebook
Website: www.samanthacoleauthor.com
Newsletter: www.geni.us/SCNews

- facebook.com/SamanthaColeAuthor
- instagram.com/samanthacoleauthor
- bookbub.com/profile/samantha-a-cole
- goodreads.com/SamanthaCole
- amazon.com/Samantha-A-Cole/e/B00X53K3X8